A BELATED DISCOVERY

THE PARABLES
BOOK 2

KENNETH A. WINTER

WildernessLessons

JOIN MY READERS' GROUP FOR UPDATES AND FUTURE RELEASES

Please join my Readers' Group so i can send you a free book, as well as updates and information about future releases, etc.

See the back of the book for details on how to sign up.

～

A Belated Discovery

A Novel

Book 2 in the series, *The Parables*

Published by:

Kenneth A. Winter

WildernessLessons, LLC

Richmond, Virginia

United States of America

kenwinter.org

wildernesslessons.com

Edited by Sheryl Martin Hash

Cover design by Scott Campbell Design

ISBN 978-1-9568663-3-9 (hard cover)

ISBN 978-1-9568663-4-6 (paperback)

ISBN 978-1-9568663-5-3 (e-book)

ISBN 978-1-9568663-6-0 (large print)

Library of Congress Control Number: 2024908644

DEDICATION

*To those who have fought and labored
in the past and in the present
to defend and safeguard the rights and freedoms
of all people.*

∾

*But let justice roll down like waters,
and righteousness like an ever-flowing stream.*

Amos 5:24 (ESV)

∾

CONTENTS

PROLOGUE

～

*T*rain number 52 pulled into the passenger station in Williamsport, Pennsylvania at five minutes before three on the afternoon of Friday, May 31. R. Eugene Fearsithe, better known as Gene to his friends, stepped off the train, sporting his brand new, custom-tailored suit.

His departure two months earlier to pursue his dream in Portland, Oregon had caused great heartbreak to the two most important people in his life. He now anxiously scanned the crowd, hoping his girlfriend, Sara, and his father, Robert, had received his telegram. Gene's pace quickened the moment he saw them.

He presented Sara with the bouquet of daisies he had purchased at the brief stop in Loch Haven. By the delighted expression on her face, you would have thought they were a dozen, long-stemmed red roses! But Gene knew daisies were her favorite flower. Robert smiled as he watched his son and Sara embrace. He was glad his son had finally come to his senses—though he would never say as much.

Gene turned to his father and repeated the same words he had just spoken to Sara: "I am so sorry for the pain I have caused you. Please forgive me."

Robert hugged his son and replied, "Gene, you were lost and now you are found. Tonight we will celebrate, because God has brought you back to us!"

Gene settled back into life in Williamsport over the next several weeks, but there was no denying he was a changed man. His father, together with the other two partners at Keller and Company, immediately recognized how his experience working for the Oregon and Washington Railroad and Navigation Company (OWR&N) had greatly sharpened his business skills. Even Sara's father, Richard Mueller, one of the other two partners, quickly became convinced Gene was not the same man as the one who left for Portland.

The three partners soon embraced many of Gene's innovative ideas, including his recommendation to enter into the emerging, all-brick-wall design of boilers. This product line enabled the company to compete in a new market—the growing number of utility companies being formed across the Northeast. Gene was so successful spearheading the sales and marketing efforts of the company, that he was soon invited to become a fourth partner.

But the changes in Gene extended beyond his prowess in business. He quickly became an active member of Memorial Baptist Church, adding his rich baritone voice to the choir. Sara didn't quite know what to make of this change, but she decided to give it a chance. After all, it was part of the journey that led Gene back to her. She faithfully joined him at church every Sunday morning and Wednesday night.

Four months after returning home, Gene asked Sara to marry him—after receiving her father's permission, of course! They were married on June 14 the following year and settled into a comfortably-sized bungalow on High Street, halfway between the church and the offices of Keller and Company. Sara continued working as a salesclerk at L.L. Stearns and Sons, the largest, family-owned and operated department store in the U.S. at the time.

Surprisingly, neither the incumbent William Howard Taft, running as the Republican candidate, nor the popular Teddy Roosevelt, running as the Progressive Party candidate, had won the election for U.S. President in 1912. Because the two men had divided the Republican vote, Woodrow Wilson became the first southern born politician to be elected as president since the years leading up to the Civil War.

When World War I broke out during the summer of 1914, President Wilson led the U.S. in remaining neutral—despite growing tensions—including the deaths of 120 U.S. passengers on the British ocean liner Lusitania, which was sunk by a German submarine on May 7, 1915.

The U.S. ultimately declared war on Germany on April 6, 1917, after realizing the country could no longer remain neutral. Within a few months, tens of thousands of men either enlisted or were drafted into the military —including Gene Fearsithe. Eventually, more than four million troops were deployed to Europe to encounter a war unlike any other that had preceded it – one waged in trenches and in the air, and one marked by the rise of such military technologies as the tank, the field telephone, and poison gas.

General John Joseph "Black Jack" Pershing was named commander of the newly created American Expeditionary Forces (AEF) stationed in France. Pershing and his staff soon realized how ill-prepared the U.S. was to transport masses of soldiers and equipment to the front, where everything was in short supply. Transport ships taking American troops to Europe were scarce, so the Army commandeered cruise ships, seized German ships, and borrowed Allied ships to transport soldiers from New York, New Jersey, and Virginia.

The mobilization effort taxed the limits of the American military and required new organizational strategies to transport troops and supplies efficiently. And that was an area where Gene could shine! His abilities were quickly recognized as critical to that effort. He was immediately given the rank of lieutenant and deployed to Hoboken, New Jersey, to lead the efforts there. Before long, he was promoted to the rank of captain.

Throughout the remainder of 1917 and into 1918, American divisions primarily augmented French and British units defending their lines and staging attacks on German positions. Captain Fearsithe was deployed to Europe in August to join the American First Army under Pershing's command. Gene's skills were put to an even greater test as he oversaw the massive logistics required to mobilize seven divisions—comprised of more than 500,000 men—in the largest offensive operation ever undertaken by U.S. armed forces.

By the time Germany signed the Armistice on November 11, 1918, the AEF had evolved into a modern, combat-tested Army recognized as one of the best in the world. But that came at a great cost. The U.S. had sustained more than 320,000 casualties; thankfully, Gene was not among them.

There was no denying as the men returned from Europe that the war had reshaped the culture of the U.S. The months that followed saw a wave of civil rights activism for equal rights for Negroes, the passage of an amendment securing the right of women to vote, and a larger role in world affairs for the U.S.

However, Gene returned home to Sara and his position at Keller and Company in time to face a battle of a different sort—an economic war. The global economy declined immediately following the conclusion of the war in Europe, and the financial boom everyone had expected to follow the war did not materialize.

As a result, the job market could not absorb the surge in the civilian labor force resulting from returning troops. It was further compounded by the arrival of a deadly influenza pandemic—the Spanish flu—that was believed to be one of the deadliest in history.

Projects that had been put on hold until after the war were now being placed on an indefinite hold. Things did not look good for Keller and Company.. But Gene knew there were always new opportunities if you were willing to look beyond the status quo. The company had never competed in the marine boiler market, since its location in Central Pennsylvania was a detriment to its ability to be competitive.

However, Gene had learned three important facts during his time in the army. First, he knew that the U.S.'s increased role in world affairs would result in a large scale expansion of the Navy for transport, as well as naval engagement. Second, he had developed strong relationships with the major U.S. shipwrights through his work in mobilizing those companies to rapidly build and launch the ships needed to transport our troops to Europe and back. Third, his ability to effect efficient transport of manpower and supplies would now provide him with the knowledge needed to ship Keller materials competitively and efficiently to the shipwrights by rail and by barge using the Susquehanna River.

Keller and Company soon became the second-largest supplier of oil-firing marine boilers on the East Coast. It also enjoyed the most profitable years to that point in the company's history. In recognition of his successful leadership, Gene was named president of the company in 1922 at the age of thirty-three.

That year also brought another cause for celebration. Sara gave birth to me, and the happy couple named me Robert Eugene Fearsithe, Jr. My dad told everyone who would listen that my birthdate—February 22—had two important distinctions. First, it was George Washington's birthday, which was an indication I was destined for greatness. Second, it is a palindrome

—2-22-22—which meant that anyone born on that date would always be distinctive.

My dad also decided that I would go by my given name, Robert, and not my middle name, so as not to create any confusion between the two of us. However, my mother thought "Robert" was too formal, so she began to call me "Bobby," and the name stuck!

Once I became old enough to consider such things, I wanted to be a baseball player. I not only loved playing the game, but knew most everything there was to know about the big-name players—Jimmie Foxx, Lefty O'Doul, Lou Gehrig, and, of course, the infamous Babe Ruth. I could tell you their batting averages, their lifetime home runs, and RBIs. My baseball glove was always within reaching distance, much to my mother's chagrin.

No organized teams for kids to play ball existed back then, so my friends and I just grabbed our gloves, a bat and ball, and found a vacant lot. We loved the game! During the summer, we would play from the time we got our chores done until sundown, with an obligatory break for supper.

The whole country appeared to love baseball. It seemed to take people's minds off the hardships brought about by the Great Depression. I was seven years old when it began, but the economic slump lasted throughout my adolescence. Even Keller and Company experienced some lean years.

In the summer of 1936, my dad announced that I needed to get a part-time job to help prepare me for adulthood. He had worked for his father at Keller and Company when he was my age, but we both agreed it was best if I worked elsewhere—somewhere I wasn't the boss's son. So he arranged for me to go to work for his Army buddy, Richard Lundy, whose business was located in the city.

Mr. Lundy, his father Frank, and his cousin Jack owned Lundy Lumber Company. I was placed under Mr. Lundy's charge and spent the summer doing miscellaneous tasks and learning everything I could about the business. After a woeful six years following the Depression, new construction in Williamsport was finally on the rebound. Remodeling work, particularly out on Millionaires' Row, was flourishing, so the lumber trade was on the increase. By the end of the summer, I was two inches taller, had added some muscle to my frame, and was able to set aside a few dollars for my future.

During the school year, my dad allowed me to work on Saturdays for Mr. Lundy. When summer arrived, though, I was back in the lumber yard almost every day. It became harder and harder to make time for baseball with my friends.

When the spring of 1939 rolled around, Mr. Lundy allowed me to work on the sales counter each Saturday. I started using the lumber knowledge I'd gleaned over the years to help customers place their orders. It also was that spring when Mr. Lundy was approached by Carl Stotz, a local man who had come up with an idea to organize a baseball league for boys. He called it Little League Baseball. Mr. Stotz's vision was for boys to have uniforms, play on a dedicated field, and use appropriately sized bats and balls just like the big leaguers!

At seventeen, I was too old to play on the teams, but I was excited about what Mr. Stotz was doing. Mr. Lundy agreed to sponsor one of the three teams—the other two were sponsored by Lycoming Dairy and Jumbo Pretzel. George Bebble was chosen to manage and coach the Lundy team. Since Mr. Lundy knew I loved baseball, he asked if I wanted to help Mr. Bebble with the team. He didn't need to ask me twice. I jumped at the chance!

Though our team didn't take home the title that first season, we did learn how to work together and encourage one another. Most of us recognized that what we were learning on that field would carry us through life, whatever the circumstances.

Two weeks after the season ended, I began my senior year at Williamsport High School. During that same period, Nazi Germany invaded Poland; the United Kingdom, France, New Zealand, and Australia declared war on Germany. President Franklin Roosevelt vowed he would make every effort to keep our country out of the conflict.

A week before my graduation ceremony, a massive evacuation of British forces took place at Dunkirk in northern France. Given my dad's role in arranging transport for our troops in the first war, he continued to comment about the massiveness of that effort. But as Prime Minister Churchill reminded his nation, "We must be very careful not to assign to this deliverance the attributes of a victory. Wars are not won by evacuations."[1]

That fall, I began my freshman year at the Williamsport Dickinson Seminary and Junior College, my dad's alma mater. But students were more preoccupied with the prospects of entering the war in Europe than we were our academic pursuits. President Roosevelt had pledged to send aid to Great Britain, declaring that the U.S. must become "the great arsenal of democracy."[2]

The national debate over whether we should come to the aid of our allies in Europe continued throughout 1941. That September, I began my second year of studies in pursuit of an associate degree in business administration.

However, on December 7, the world as we knew it changed forever. Japan launched a surprise attack on the U.S. fleet at Pearl Harbor in Hawaii, and Germany was threatening to declare war on us. The decision about entering the war had been made for us.

And I knew it was time to put my studies on hold.

~

[1] From Winston Churchill's address to the House of Commons on June 4, 1940

https://winstonchurchill.org/resources/speeches/1940-the-finest-hour/we-shall-fight-on-the-beaches/

[2] From a Fireside Chat delivered by Franklin D. Roosevelt to the nation on December 29, 1940

1

THURSDAY, DECEMBER 11 – MONDAY, DECEMBER 15, 1941

~

To the Congress:

On the morning of December eleventh, the Government of Germany, pursuing its course of world conquest, declared war against the United States.

The long known and the long expected has thus taken place. The forces endeavoring to enslave the entire world now are moving toward this hemisphere.

Never before has there been a greater challenge to life, liberty, and civilization.

Delay invites greater danger. Rapid and united effort by all of the peoples of the world who are determined to remain free will insure a world victory of the forces of justice and of righteousness over the forces of savagery and of barbarism.

Italy also has declared war against the United States.

I therefore request the Congress to recognize a state of war between the United States and Germany, and between the United States and Italy.

President Franklin D. Roosevelt[1]

. . .

*T*hough we knew the arrival of this day was inevitable, we were still shocked by events over the past week. Our nation had been stunned by the Empire of Japan's unprovoked attack on Pearl Harbor, resulting in the devastating loss of American lives as well as naval ships. Four days later, Adolf Hitler and Benito Mussolini declared war on the U.S.

Congress immediately responded to President Roosevelt's request and issued a declaration of war on Germany and Italy. We were now fully engaged on both fronts.

As my parents and I sat down to dinner that evening, we realized that life as we knew it would never be the same. Another world war was all anyone could talk about. Many of our friends and neighbors believed we should have acted sooner, but that was now a moot point.

"I stopped by city hall this afternoon," I announced, "and spoke with two Army representatives who set up a recruiting station there."

Neither of my parents was surprised. Though my mother was hesitant to see her son go off to war, she also knew it was the right thing to do. I had no doubt my father would be supportive.

"I informed the officers I would like to enroll in infantry officer candidate school (OCS) at Fort Benning, Georgia. They said I met all the necessary requirements except the minimum age, which is twenty-one. Dad, do you think one of your contacts in the Army could arrange an exception for me?"

"I think we can make a strong case, given your education and your super-visory experience at Lundy's," my father replied. "Our military has a tremendous need for new officers now. Since OCS is still relatively new, I think we may get a favorable answer from the powers that be in Washington. I'll put in a call first thing in the morning."

What my father didn't tell me was he would be contacting Brigadier General Leonard Gerow! General Gerow was the Chief of War Plans Division of the War Department general staff. He and my father had worked together as captains under General Pershing.

General Gerow's career path had intersected with Brigadier General Omar Bradley's throughout the years. They had attended an advance course at the Infantry School at Fort Benning and graduated first and second in their class, respectively. General Bradley had been given command over the Infantry OCS at Fort Benning.

The OCS had graduated 171 second lieutenants earlier that fall, but the declaration of war meant officers needed to be trained more rapidly. Nonetheless, there was already a long waiting list of candidates. The soonest I could attend was the beginning of April, after completing basic training. But the two recruiters had told me the April classes were most assuredly already full.

I could hardly concentrate on anything else as I waited for a response to my father's call. On Saturday morning, I received a telephone call at the lumberyard from Captain John Throckmorton, an aide to General Bradley.

"Fearsithe," he began, "you appear to have valuable connections. We are holding a place for you in the twenty-seventh OSC class beginning April 6. However, you need to do two things immediately. Go to your local recruiting office Monday morning and put in your enlistment papers. You will be expected at the thirteen-week basic training at Fort Benning that begins the second of January.

"Next, complete the application for OCS and make sure it is in my hands by the end of this coming week. Any delays will forfeit your space in the

OCS. And obviously, final approval is subject to the review of your application and the satisfactory completion of your basic training. Do you have any questions?"

"No, sir, I do not," I replied.

"Good. And Fearsithe, this is the only exception your connections will get you. From here on, you need to earn your spot, son! Am I clear?"

"Yes, sir!" I replied, a moment before the call ended.

I immediately gave my notice to Mr. Lundy and asked him to write a letter of recommendation so I could include it with my application for OCS. Mine was the fifth resignation Mr. Lundy had received that week as men of all ages responded to the call to fight for our country.

Like most people across the U.S., I felt the need to be in a place of worship that weekend. My parents and I made our way through the accumulating snowfall to attend the Sunday morning service at Memorial Baptist Church in Newberry. After a somber rendition of "Onward, Christian Soldiers," Pastor Harold Peterson led the congregation in prayer:

"Dear Heavenly Father, as we face the challenges of war, we seek your guidance and strength to navigate through this difficult period. We pray for our leaders and soldiers as they take on this responsibility. Grant us the courage to stand united as a nation and the compassion to support those affected by this conflict. In Jesus's name, Amen.

"Today we come together with heavy hearts but also a renewed sense of purpose. Our beloved nation has been thrust into a global conflict, facing the forces of darkness and evil. As followers of Christ, we are called to respond with courage, faith, and unwavering resolve. Let us reflect on

God's Word and find strength in His promises as we navigate through these challenging times.

"In Ecclesiastes 3:8, we are reminded that there is 'a time for war and a time for peace.' Today, we find ourselves in the midst of such a time, a time to stand against the forces that threaten the freedom and peace we cherish. Our nation has been attacked, and we must rise to the challenge with courage and determination.

"As we confront this new reality, we must seek God's guidance and wisdom. Let us remember to pray for our leaders and the men and women in uniform. May God's wisdom guide their decisions and actions.

"And let us exemplify Christ's love by supporting one another and extending compassion to those affected by this conflict. Our prayers and actions can make a significant difference in the lives of those around us.

"As we face this time of uncertainty, let us continue to hold fast to the hope that God has a purpose for us—individually, and as a nation. Our faith in God's plan will sustain us through the darkest hours.

"Let us not be driven by fear but rather be motivated by faith. As we face the challenges ahead, let us be bold in defending what is right, just, and true. Let us love and support one another, standing united as a nation and placing our hope in the sovereign God who guides us through all trials.

"And lastly, may we, as a church and as a nation, be known for our unwavering faith, compassion, and resilience. May the peace of God, which surpasses all understanding, guard our hearts and minds in Christ Jesus."

The service concluded with all of us singing the recently penned hymn by Irving Berlin, "God Bless America."

Pastor Peterson greeted each of us at the door as we exited the church. When it was our turn to file past him, he shook my hand and said, "Bobby, your parents tell me you plan to enlist tomorrow. Thank you for your willingness to serve. Know that your pastor and your church will be praying for you—for courage, for strength, and for protection—as you defend the freedoms and the peace we all cherish."

"Thank you, pastor. I'll take all the prayers I can get, and I'll trust the Good Lord to favor those of us who fight for the side that's right!"

As my parents and I walked to the car, we ran into one of my buddies, Rob Smith. I was about an inch taller than Rob, but he had me beat by fifty pounds in weight—and it was all muscle. He had played lineman on our high school football team and could bench press 300 pounds at the time. He hadn't changed a bit. His blond hair and rugged good looks had always made him a favorite with the ladies.

Rob and I had been friends since kindergarten, but I hadn't seen much of him since we graduated. As a matter of fact, I hadn't seen him at church for a long time.

"Bobby, did I hear you plan to enlist tomorrow?" he asked.

"I sure am. Boy, news sure travels fast around here."

"Yeah, it does," he laughed. "I'm planning on doing the same, and I expect a few of the other boys will be joining us as well."

"I guess that means I'll be seeing you tomorrow, then," I responded. "Enjoy the rest of your day at home with your family. Pretty soon, we'll probably wish we could enjoy more of those days."

"Yeah, you're right," he said as he scurried off to catch up with his family. "I'll look for you tomorrow, Bobby," he yelled over his shoulder.

Mom was fixing one of my favorite meals for Sunday dinner—beef roast with mashed potatoes and gravy. We could smell the aroma coming from the kitchen as soon as we opened the door. The snow had stopped while we were driving home, and the clouds were starting to clear. It looked to be about three inches on the ground—just enough to make everything look clean and white.

After dinner, Dad and I sat in the living room reading the newspaper and listening to the radio. Romania, Bulgaria, and Hungary had just declared war on both Great Britain and the U.S., and our nations had responded in kind. It seemed as if everyone was choosing a side. I couldn't imagine anyone remaining neutral in this fight—even though the U.S. had done so until now … probably for longer than we should have.

Later that afternoon, there was a knock at our front door. My longtime friend and next-door neighbor, Donny Busey, was standing there—all five foot, four inches of him. Our families had lived beside each other since he and I were five years old. Other than being the same age, though, we had little in common. Donny had always been the brainiest kid in school, but his diminutive stature had made him socially and physically awkward. He struggled to make friends and became a bit of a recluse after high school. However, he had always felt comfortable with me.

"Hey, Bobby," he said. "Mind if I talk to you for a minute?"

"Sure, Donny. Come on in!"

"Well, I was wondering if maybe you could come outside and we could go for a walk or something. I'd rather have this conversation where others can't hear us. Is that okay?"

Over the years, he had asked me to come outside for a number of "private" conversations. Most often, they had to do with matters of the heart—whether he should ask a girl to go to a dance—or matters of the intellect, like whether he should try out for the high school debate team. I actually was honored he thought so highly of my opinion.

"Let me grab my coat and scarf," I told him.

"Bobby, I know you and some of the other guys are planning to enlist in the Army," he began once we were safely out of earshot. "Others are saying they're going to wait until they're drafted. My parents think that's what I should do, but I'm not sure.

"My dad told me I was too short to enlist, but I spoke with the recruiter at City Hall and he told me the minimum height requirement is five feet. Mom said they wouldn't take me because I wear glasses, but the officer had me read his eye chart and told me I would pass. I think my parents are just scared."

"Well, of course they're scared, Donny! That's normal when their son is volunteering to go into harm's way. They're just trying to put it off as long as they can. But what do you think?"

"I think I need to go and fight for my country," Donny stated. "I know I'm not as big and strong as guys like you, but sometimes it's the little wiry ones who can get into places that others can't. Besides, I'm sure the Army will train me in all I need to know."

"Well, it sounds to me like you've made up your mind. Now you just need to tell your parents."

"Yeah, it does," Donny agreed. "But that's the hard part. I know my mom will cry, and my dad will probably yell at me."

"I don't think so," I countered. "You just need to tell them how you feel. Remind them that young men have been fighting to defend the freedoms we enjoy since this nation was founded. And now it's your turn!

"After all, that's the man your parents raised you to be—one who does what needs to be done. I believe they'll come around to your way of thinking. That's not to say your mom won't cry. I expect my mom's already shed some tears. But your dad won't shout. Actually, I think he'll be proud of you."

"You think so, Bobby?"

"Yeah, Donny, I sure do."

"Well then, that's what I'll do," Donny declared. "So I'll probably see you at the recruiting station first thing in the morning. Thanks for helping me talk this through, Bobby."

"It's all copacetic! And we'll probably go to basic training together—so it will be my honor to serve with you."

Donny smiled, gave me a salute that would never pass muster, and headed back to his house. Bravery comes in all shapes and sizes; Donny Busey was proof of that.

I stepped back into the warmth of my home and decided to challenge my parents to a hand or two of gin rummy. They loved a good game of cards, so I knew they wouldn't be able to resist. We played and laughed into the night. I don't think we kept score—we just enjoyed spending time together.

Rob, Donny, and I entered the recruiting office together the next morning as soon as the doors opened. In short order, the recruiters took us through the paces of enlistment.

"Fearsithe, you most definitely have some pull in D.C.," Sergeant McCracken said as soon as he filled out my paperwork. "I received a call about you earlier this morning."

"Yes, sergeant," I answered. "I understand I am supposed to report to Fort Benning two weeks from Friday."

"Actually, soldier, your schedule just got moved up. You are to report here two days earlier," the sergeant replied. "With you three fellows and the others who have already signed up, we now have enough young men enlisted here in Williamsport to fill at least two buses. You all will be leaving at 2:00 p.m. on Wednesday, December 31. Plan to ring in the new year with your fellow soldiers.

"Also, I have been told to give you this application for OCS. You are to complete it and return it to me by 5:00 p.m. the day after tomorrow, so I can get it to Fort Benning by Friday. Apparently, subject to its review, you have been bumped up the list to join the OCS class that starts the beginning of April—provided you survive basic training. Make sure you get your paperwork back to me on time."

"Yes, sergeant!"

∾

---

[1] Speech delivered by President Franklin D. Roosevelt to Congress on December 11, 1941, National Archives

2

TUESDAY, DECEMBER 16, 1941 – THURSDAY MORNING, JANUARY 1, 1942

❧

I spent the next two days assembling the documents needed to accompany my OCS application: a signed form from Doc Foster certifying my physical fitness plus my medical history; a copy of my high school transcript; a transcript of my studies from my three semesters at Dickinson Junior College, and my letters of recommendation.

Mr. Lundy's letter vouched for my work ethic during my employment at Lundy Lumber Company. Mr. Bebble, manager of the Little League baseball team, wrote about my ability to lead men in a team effort—albeit teenage men. I also included a letter from Pastor Peterson that spoke to my moral character.

The next step was taking several written tests that evaluated my ability to think under pressure in the midst of various situations with a mixture of personality types. I was also required to include a typed essay on why I wanted to become an Army officer and how that related to my future goals. By the time I was done, the Army knew more about me than I knew about myself!

Finally, I was able to hand over the completed application packet to Sergeant McCracken at 4:45 p.m. Wednesday.

"Fearsithe, I think you may have just passed your first test," the sergeant grinned as he looked up at the wall clock. "I've never seen anyone pull together all the information required in less than two weeks, and you did it in under three days—with fifteen minutes to spare. Good job, soldier!"

There wasn't much more to do before my departure, so I spent most of the week before Christmas working at Lundy's. Business was steady but not brisk. The mood at the store matched that of the entire city. We were mourning the deaths of those who had lost their lives in Pearl Harbor, but there also was an increased sense of patriotism and unity.

I received more backslaps, "attaboys," and "we're-proud-of you-sons" than I could count as more people learned I was headed to Fort Benning at the end of the month. Complete strangers would come up and shake my hand, saying they were praying for all of us young men headed to war.

But coupled with national pride was a lot of anxiety and uncertainty. No one knew how this global conflict would impact his or her life. However, our nation understood it would require sacrifice and a commitment to do whatever was needed to win the war. Though many families were trying to hold onto their holiday traditions, peace and goodwill had taken on different meanings—and joy was now a possession to treasure and cherish.

Churches across the country were filled with people seeking a sense of hope that Christmas season. Hymns like "Joy to the World" and "Silent Night" became reverent prayers as their words took on deeper meaning.

In an effort to maintain some sense of normalcy, my parents held to their Christmas Eve tradition of serving my mother's famous chili con carne to friends who dropped by after the evening church service. Donny Busey and his parents joined us as they did each year, and I could tell his parents weren't quite yet at peace with his decision to enlist.

"You keep an eye on my son, Bobby," his mother whispered to me at one point. "He looks up to you, and he thinks he needs to do whatever you do. Bring him home to me, Bobby."

I suddenly felt the weight of that burden, one I hadn't considered. I knew I may not return from war—but I hadn't yet considered the future of my friends and the men who would be under my command.

"With the good Lord's help, I'll do my best," I assured her.

Her sad eyes conveyed the words she couldn't say out loud before she silently walked back to her husband. I ambled over to a corner of the living room where several men from my father's company were shooting the breeze.

"Gene was on the telephone this morning with Admiral Robinson, director of the Navy's newly created office of procurement and material," Jim Frazier, one of the company partners, was saying. He had taken over Grandpa Fearsithe's position on the management team after he retired.

"The admiral is another one of the bigwigs Gene knows from his time in the military," Jim continued. "Apparently, we're about to undergo a significant retooling of our manufacturing plant—again."

Jim switched topics when he realized I had joined them. "And now we're also about to deploy one of our best and brightest to the front lines," he added. "When do you head out, Bobby?"

"If everything goes as planned, a number of us Williamsport fellows will head out a week from today for basic training at Fort Benning. After that, I will begin Officer Candidate School for another ninety days, so I don't expect to make my way overseas for another six to seven months."

"Well, we thank you for your willingness to serve, and we're certain you will do us all proud, just like your father did," Jim replied, as the other men nodded in agreement.

My mother seldom missed Bing Crosby's radio program, and Christmas Eve was no exception. The crooner's rich baritone voice was serenading us in the background with familiar Christmas carols. Suddenly, he introduced a new song that caught everyone's attention. Mom walked over to the Marconi console and turned up the volume. Our friends fell silent as we all listened to "White Christmas," written by composer Irving Berlin, for the first time.

The lyrics, sung in the way only Bing can, harkened us back to Christ-mases out from under the clouds of war. Before the song was finished, most of us had joined in with Bing on the final refrain. It seemed to be the right note on which to conclude the evening.

Our quiet, traditional Christmas dinner featured roast turkey and stuffing —but this year there were only three of us gathered at the table. Both of my grandfathers usually joined us for the holiday, but my mother's dad died suddenly of a heart attack in February, and my father's dad had passed in July after a prolonged illness. Grandpa Fearsithe had lived with us for six months leading up to his death. My dad and I simultaneously looked over at the empty chair he had occupied.

I took mental "snapshots" that day so I could recall them later: mom preparing our holiday feast in the kitchen, my family around the dinner table, and my dad unwrapping his gift in front of the Christmas tree. I knew we were all thinking the same thing—this could well be my last Christmas at home for quite a while.

Each day after that was a day of "lasts." Sunday was my last time to worship at my church. Pastor Peterson's message was especially moving and inspiring. At the end of the service, he called Rob Smith and me to the altar so the congregation could pray over us.

"Heavenly Father," the pastor began, "You know these young men. They are Your young men. They are like the mighty men of King David, going out to engage in battle with those who have declared themselves to be our enemies. They fight for the cause that is right and just. They have already shown their bravery by choosing to be among the first men to go. They have stepped out declaring their faith and trust in You.

"Lord, as both of these men leave us—not only to fight, but also to serve as leaders among their fellow soldiers—we ask that You enable them to fight valiantly and to lead courageously. We pray that You would keep them from harm and bring them back to us safely once victory has been accomplished.

"Lord, those of us who remain on these shores commit to lift these young men in prayer as long as this war lasts, just as Aaron and Hur did as the battle raged between Your people and the Amalekites. We commit to watch over their families and minister to any needs that arise as they await the return of their sons.

"And we pray, Lord, that You would enable victory to come quickly . . . for right to prevail . . . and for a peace to return to this land that brings glory to You. In Jesus's name we pray, Amen!"

It was a slow day at work Monday, which gave me time to say farewell to my fellow employees and customers who had become friends. Some would soon be joining me in the fight—and a few had already gone.

Mr. Lundy shook my hand and said, "Bobby, I know you are destined for great things—both as you serve this nation during wartime and once the fighting is done. I expect you will have a number of great opportunities when you return home, but know you always have a place here if you need it."

Tuesday night was my last meal with my parents. My mom prepared all my favorite foods. She even baked a peanut butter cake with peanut butter frosting for dessert—and packed the leftovers for me to take on the bus.

My parents took me to the bus station Wednesday afternoon to see me off. We had said our goodbyes at home, so all that was left was a final embrace. Mom had done well holding back her tears—until that moment. But I was ready; I had brought an extra handkerchief just for the occasion.

Before I got on the bus, my dad hugged me and prayed over me: "Lord, he's Yours! You've entrusted him to us these nineteen years, but he's always been Yours. We've protected him as best we can, but now it's all on You. Keep him from harm, and bring him back to us in one piece."

Mom and Dad waved as the bus pulled away, and I prayed, "And Lord, keep my parents from undue worry and keep them safe while I'm gone. I'm not going to be here to watch over them—so it's all on You!"

Donny sat in the seat beside me, Rob was in the seat behind me, and seventeen other guys were scattered throughout the bus. Some of them I knew. Doug Fessler and I had been in Junior Rotary together in high school. Rick Gordon was a year ahead of me, but he and I had been in glee club together for a couple of years. Jack Schrader and I had worked in the lumberyard at Lundy's for a couple of summers. And a few of the others looked familiar, though I didn't know their names.

About 7:30 p.m., we pulled into the parking lot of a café in Fredericksburg, Virginia. Another bus from the same company as ours was already parked there. But I was surprised to find the restaurant empty except for the man who obviously was the other bus driver. The restaurant staff apparently expected us because they told us where the men's room was and ushered us to our tables.

It was a delicious meal—my first introduction to Southern cooking—served family style. You'd have thought we hadn't eaten in a week the way we devoured the fried chicken, black-eyed peas, collard greens, and mashed potatoes. The waitresses served up pitcher after pitcher of sweet tea to wash it all down and sweet potato pie for dessert.

The hunger pangs gnawing at my stomach for the past few hours were a distant memory as I finally pushed back from the table. I think the other guys felt the same way; the only sound was the clatter of forks against plates as we shoveled in food—lots of food. After forty minutes, our driver announced it was time to get back on the road.

Once outside, I noticed a group of men waiting to board the second bus, though I had not seen them inside the café. As I got closer, I realized they were all colored. They were staring at us and we at them.

I suddenly realized I knew one of the men.

"Larnell, is that you?" I asked. "What are you doing here?"

Larnell Williams and I had worked together in the lumberyard during the past year. We had briefly spoken on a few occasions.

"I expect I'm doing the same thing you are, Mr. Bobby," he replied.

"Are all of you traveling from Williamsport to Fort Benning for basic training as well?"

"Well, we're all headed from Williamsport, same as you," Larnell answered. "And we've all enlisted to fight for our country just like you. But we're headed to Camp Lee, outside of Petersburg, Virginia, for our basic training."

"I wonder why you're going to Camp Lee and we're going to Fort Benning," I thought out loud.

"Because Camp Lee is where they train Negro soldiers," Larnell replied.

"I didn't know that, Larnell. And come to think of it, where were all of you while we were inside eating dinner? Have you been fed?"

"Yes, we've eaten. They had a special place for us out back, just behind the back door of the kitchen."

I suddenly realized I was being confronted by something I had always known existed—though I never talked about it, and I most definitely hadn't given it much thought. Just then the driver of my bus called out, "Come along now and get on the bus. We've got to be pulling out."

I gave Larnell a nod and the two of us moved on. But I felt compelled to turn back and call out, "You take care of yourself, Larnell."

"You too, Mr. Bobby."

Just south of Richmond, Virginia, we cut over to U.S. Highway 460, which eventually ran parallel to the Appalachian Trail. If it hadn't been night-time, it would have been a scenic ride over the Shenandoah Valley and through the Appalachian Mountains. Between our full stomachs and the rhythmic sound of the wheels on the highway, it wasn't long before the bus was filled with melodious snoring. However, thoughts about Larnell and those other men kept me from nodding off.

A few minutes before midnight the driver called out, "Men, the ball won't be dropping in Times Square to ring in the new year due to the wartime dimout of lights in New York City. Instead, people gathered there will observe one minute of silence, followed by the ringing of chimes.

"I'm sure most of you men are away from your families and friends this New Year's Eve for the first time. Would you be willing to join me in singing "Auld Lang Syne" to ring in this next year—whatever it may bring?"

"Of course we will!" I shouted in reply. "Rick, let's put our glee club experience to good use."

Rick and I led the men in a reflective rendition of the song. It was obvious we were all wondering what this new year might hold for us, for our families, and for our nation. When we finished singing, there was no rousing cheer to ring in the year—only silence.

After a few moments, the driver called out, "God bless you men! May He keep you safe."

Pretty soon the only sound in the bus was a chorus of snores.

∾

3

THURSDAY AFTERNOON, JANUARY 1 – FRIDAY, JANUARY 2, 1942

~

Our bus pulled up to the reception area of Fort Benning at three o'clock in the afternoon, or as we were soon to be reminded, at 1500 hours. A Sergeant O'Reilly climbed onto our bus and introduced himself in a voice that clearly commanded our attention.

"Welcome to Fort Benning, men!" he called out. "I will be your training sergeant during your time here. There is very little you will do for the next twelve weeks that is without my instruction or permission. My job is to turn you into infantrymen in the U.S. Army, and I can see I have my work cut out for me!

"On my command, you will disembark in a few moments, carrying whatever personal items you have. You will form a line, standing at attention, in four rows of five with three feet between you and the soldiers around you. Make sure your rows and your lines are straight.

"When I issue that command, you will reply, 'Yes, sergeant!' and then immediately obey. If you listen to my orders, respond at once, and then carry them out as instructed, you should do well in basic training.

"Disembark and fall in!" he shouted.

"Yes, sergeant!" rang out from most of us, with a few "Yes, sirs!" sprinkled in. Before we left our seats, the sergeant shouted, "Sit down!"

Again most of us replied, "Yes, sergeant!" but several guys still responded with "Yes, sir!"—including Donny. Sergeant O'Reilly strode to where Donny and I were sitting and glared down at him.

"What is your name, soldier?" the sergeant demanded.

"Donny Busey, sir!" Donny nervously replied.

"Private Busey, what does this chevron on my upper sleeve indicate to you?"

"It means you are a sergeant, sir!" Donny replied with confidence.

"You are half correct, Private Busey. But being half correct means you are very wrong. I am a sergeant—a rank I hold with pride as a non-commissioned officer. But I am not a 'sergeant, sir.' The title 'sir' refers to a commissioned officer."

The sergeant's voice rose in volume. "I am not your papa, your mama, or a sir. You will refer to me as sergeant. Is that clear Private Busey?"

"Yes, sergeant!" Donny replied.

"And is that clear to the rest of you?" the sergeant shouted.

"Yes, sergeant!" we replied in unison.

"Now, disembark and fall in!" he shouted once more.

"Yes, sergeant!"

Though we had learned how to reply to our sergeant, it was quickly apparent that our ability to line up in rows as instructed was going to take some practice. As I watched the chaos unfold, I quickly decided to take charge. Within a few moments, our ragtag band of novice soldiers was standing at attention—all under the disapproving stare of Sergeant O'Reilly.

I was a little taken back when he turned to me and asked, "Private, what is your name?"

"Private Robert Fearsithe, sergeant."

"I thought as much," he responded, though I wasn't quite sure what he meant.

"Soldiers, in a few minutes I'm going to dismiss you," he said, addressing the group. "Private Fearsithe will lead his row in a straight line; those of you in the other three rows will fall in by row behind them.

"Your first stop is the reception building straight ahead. You will present the military paperwork you received when you enlisted and sign your contract. You will then be issued your dog tags, which you will wear around your neck at all times.

"Next, you will proceed to the base barbershop—where you will begin to look like real soldiers. But that is only the beginning of your wonderful transformation!

"Following your haircut, you will be directed to the depot where you will be issued your uniforms, boots, helmets, and personal gear. Once that is completed, you will again line up in single file behind Private Fearsithe and await further instructions.

"Private Fearsithe, do you have any questions?"

"No, sergeant!" I promptly replied.

"Well, in that case, soldiers, fall in!"

Obviously, the U.S. Army and Fort Benning, in particular, had become adept at receiving new recruits; they had fine-tuned the process into a well-oiled machine. We had all completed our tasks and were back in line in forty-five minutes. At 1600 hours, Sergeant O'Reilly arrived at the head of our line just as the final soldier stepped into place.

"Soldiers, your next appointment is with the base medical staff. You will follow Private Fearsithe to the exam room where the docs will put you through the paces of a thorough examination assessing your physical fitness and identifying any pre-existing medical conditions. There should be no surprises since you each underwent a physical exam by your own doctor and submitted the results to your recruiting office prior to coming here.

"Once the examination is complete, you will receive the required vaccinations and immunizations. You will then return to this place and line up in single file.

"Private Fearsithe, do you have any questions?"

"No, sergeant!" I responded.

"Soldiers, you have your orders. Step to it!"

"Yes, sergeant!"

Just like at every other stop at Fort Benning, the medical staff was quick and efficient. Even the shots were given with precision, with one medical corpsman standing on each side of us as they administered needles into both our arms simultaneously. Even those who were afraid of shots weren't given time to wince. We were now recipients of medical care the Army way!

Later that day, we were assigned our sleeping barracks and individual bunks and lockers—complete with instructions on how to make up our beds. We reported to the mess hall for dinner at 1800 hours. While we ate our first meal of Army chow, we quietly exchanged reactions about our first day of boot camp.

"Sergeant O'Reilly seemed to recognize you," Rob Smith, who was seated beside me, said between bites of meatloaf, peas, and mashed potatoes with gravy. "Have you met him before?"

"No," I replied, "but he sure did seem to recognize my name when he first saw me. I'm not sure what that's all about."

"And he called you out to lead our line," Rob continued. "He must sense that you're a natural leader."

"Either that, or he picked me because I'm the best looking," I said with a grin.

"No, that couldn't be it. It must be because you're the tallest," Rob jested, returning the grin.

"What do you guys think of him so far?" Donny asked from across the table.

"So far he's exactly what I've always heard a drill sergeant is supposed to be like—no nonsense and somewhat intimidating," I answered.

At that moment, Donny's eyes got as big as saucers as he stared over my head.

"Only somewhat intimidating, private?" Sergeant O'Reilly bellowed from behind me. "Apparently I'm going to have to work on my demeanor."

I instinctively sprang to my feet and turned to face the sergeant. I stood about four inches taller, so I actually was looking down on him. Something about that made me uncomfortable, and I took a couple of steps back.

"You three report to me at the barracks at 1845—and don't be late."

I had no idea what was about to happen, but I knew it couldn't be good. Rob, Donny, and I sat in silence as we finished our dinner. And we made sure to be a few minutes early for our appointment with the sergeant.

The sergeant entered the barracks at exactly 1845 and instructed us to follow him to the latrine.

"Privates, I noticed earlier today that this latrine is not as clean and polished as it should be. And since it's the first night you men will be spending on base, I've decided we need to make sure it is particularly clean tonight. So I want you men to make sure it shines before the rest of your fellow soldiers return to the barracks. Make sure there isn't a speck of dirt anywhere and that all the porcelain sparkles. Do I make myself completely clear or only somewhat clear, Private Fearsithe?"

"Completely clear, sergeant," I replied.

"Then get to work," he grunted.

For the next hour, the three of us scrubbed the floor, the sinks, the toilets, and the showers. I had to admit, it was probably cleaner than our bathrooms back home!

At 1955, just before the rest of the men were scheduled to return, the sergeant reappeared to inspect our work. I was half expecting him to find something out of order, but he didn't.

"Privates, I see you have made certain this latrine is completely clean and not somewhat clean. There is no room in this man's Army for anything to be referred to as 'somewhat.' If it's not complete—or completely—then it's not been done correctly. That goes for a task, an attitude, or an action. I never want you men to do anything that is referred to as 'somewhat,' and I can assure you I never want anything I do to be referred to in that manner. Have I made myself clear, privates?"

"Completely, sergeant!" we replied in unison.

We were dismissed to join the rest of the men entering the barracks. We had about an hour of personal time before the bugle sounded, signaling lights out.

As I lay on my bunk in the dark reflecting on the day, there was no question that this had been the most unusual New Year's Day that I, or any of us, had ever experienced!

Reveille sounded at 0530 the next morning. We promptly got up, made our bunks, and got ready for the day. It was cold when we assembled at 0600 on the field outside our barracks. Our squad of twenty men was combined with two other squads to make up a platoon of sixty. From there on out, we did everything as a platoon.

Our day began with calisthenics before we headed out on a forty-five minute, fast-paced run around the camp. The sergeant took the lead and, by the time we returned to the barracks, there was no question he was in better shape than all of us.

After a brief break, we gathered in the same field for morning formation. Sergeant O'Reilly informed us we would line up each morning in the same formation—three squads with each squad in four rows of five men each. Two other men and I were selected to be squad leaders.

The sergeant took us through our paces until we could gather in perfect formation in thirty seconds. He then drilled us on proper responses to common commands including attention, at ease, parade rest, right face, left face, about face, and forward march. I am sure we looked comical before we mastered our responses—but no one was laughing.

Our next lesson was learning how to march in formation, culminating in our first march to the mess hall for breakfast at 0830 hours. Nothing had ever tasted better than that meal of eggs, spam, biscuits with gravy, and coffee. As we talked among ourselves, we kept a watchful eye to make sure idle remarks weren't again overheard!

At 0900 hours, we marched to classrooms for instruction in military history, first aid, and map reading. Though I was somewhat familiar with military history from my dad and grandfather, I still found it quite interesting. Much of the first aid training was similar to what I had learned during my time at Lundy's.

Our platoon quickly discovered that you march everywhere you go in the Army! At 1200 hours, we marched back to the mess hall and feasted on beef stew with potatoes and carrots. What Army food lacked in quality, it more than made up for with quantity. I had yet to walk away hungry from a meal.

That afternoon found us marching and responding to commands the sergeant had taught us that morning. When the session finally concluded, we were exhausted. Following a thirty-minute break, we gathered for evening formation at 1700 hours. That was when we received our duty assignments for the week.

"Fearsithe, Busey, and Smith," bellowed the sergeant, "the three of you did such an excellent job on latrine duty last night, I have decided you will continue that assignment for the week. You'll be setting the standard for your fellow soldiers in how it's to be done. Report to the barracks' latrine at 1845 following evening mess. Have I made myself clear, soldiers?"

"Yes, sergeant!" the three of us shouted back in unison. "Completely clear!"

The sergeant went on to explain that the schedule we had followed for the past twenty-four hours would be our recurring schedule for our time in basic training. The morning and afternoon training sessions would vary as we transformed into soldiers who wore the U.S. Army uniform with distinction.

"We demonstrated in the last war that we are the best fighting force in the world," he added. "We're going to show Hitler, Mussolini, and Hirohito that they waged war with the wrong nation. They have pulled the tail of the wrong dog. And we're going to bite them back with vengeance and put a stop to their efforts to dominate the world!

"We will drive them back to Berlin, Rome, and Tokyo, and make them wish they had never engaged the United States. Our Navy will destroy them on the seas, our Air Force will eradicate them in the skies, and our Infantry—including you men—will beat them back on land! It is my job to make sure you are fully trained and capable of doing that. And men, I take my job very seriously, and I expect you to do the same. Do you understand?"

"Yes, sergeant, completely!" we all shouted in a thunderous response.

4

SATURDAY, JANUARY 3 – FRIDAY MORNING, APRIL 3, 1942

∿

The days soon blended into one another. Sergeant O'Reilly continued to push us harder and farther—and it was paying off. We were all in top physical shape. As the weeks passed, I sensed a change not only in my physical stamina, but also in my perspective. I was becoming a professional soldier, trained to think and act as a member of the finest military force in the world.

I had arrived at Fort Benning wanting to be trained to defeat the inhumanity and tyranny being unleased on the world by the Nazis and Japanese; but I soon realized our training was about more than that. We were being taught how to become men of principle, defending and protecting the fundamental beliefs of liberty and democracy on which our nation was formed. We had arrived as individuals—but we were becoming a band of brothers united in purpose. I couldn't help but feel proud.

I saw the same transformation in each of the men in our platoon. Though we had come from different walks of life, the training was fostering a sense of camaraderie. We had to rely on one another for support—and survival.

Sharing the physical rigors of training and the emotional challenges of being away from our families bonded us.

The changes in Donny were most noticeable. The shy, awkward kid from Williamsport was now a man, standing tall and with confidence. He was mastering the physical and mental challenges of the obstacle course and earning the respect of the platoon. I even noticed him joining in the rivalry and friendly competition among the men. All of us were being pushed to excel and exceed our personal limits.

Not surprisingly, Rob continued to demonstrate his innate leadership skills. We had both been promoted to Private First Class early in our training. Sergeant O'Reilly gave us each added responsibilities and challenged us to make sure no one was left behind in training.

Rob had definitely changed since our high school years, but I hadn't quite put my finger on just how and why until a conversation during our early days of basic training. He had confided that he felt like a rudderless boat in the ocean—he had lost his sense of purpose. But in the weeks since then, I was seeing more of the old Rob I'd always known.

On Sunday, February 8, the nation rolled all clocks ahead one hour as President Roosevelt's year-round daylight savings plan, which he called "War Time," was instituted to reduce energy consumption. It took us a few days to adjust to having an additional hour of darkness each morning, but the upside was an added hour of sunlight between afternoon training and dinnertime.

The following week, we received news that the city of Singapore had fallen and surrendered to the Japanese. Eighty thousand soldiers—British, Indian, Australian, and Singaporean—were taken prisoner. Similar stories continued to roll in about the German advance in Europe. The dominant discussion in the mess hall each night was about how much our troops were needed on both fronts to help turn the tide. Even though the brutality of the battlefield awaited us, we were impatient for training to be over and eager to be deployed.

During the sixth week of training, Rob excitedly informed me that he, too, had been accepted into OCS. Without the benefit of my father's connections in Washington, Rob had entered the application process at the rear of the line.

"Sergeant O'Reilly must have put in a good word on my behalf," Rob grinned while waving a letter in his hand. "This says I have been accepted into OCS Class 27. The sergeant told me there was only one remaining opening, and I got it. He says you and I can put in a request to room together."

"Congratulations, Rob! Who would have guessed we would be training together to become officers in the U.S. Army? I know your parents will be so proud of you!"

"Yes, I'm going to call them tonight to let them know."

"How do we put in a request to room together?" I asked.

"The sergeant said it was fairly easy since we're already here at Fort Benning. You and I can simply walk over to the OCS training office and fill out a request form. He said he was certain they would accept it."

"Well, let's do it then, by all means," I replied. "We can go tomorrow afternoon after training."

On Monday, March 9, the sergeant announced that the Army had been reorganized into three forces: Army ground forces, Army air forces, and Army service forces. Most of us just shrugged our shoulders when we talked about it later in our barracks. It wouldn't make much difference since we had always been ground forces.

That same day I was promoted to the rank of Corporal. Sergeant O'Reilly presented me with my stripes at morning roll call saying, "Men, it is highly unusual for a recruit to be promoted to a corporal at this stage of training. However, Corporal Fearsithe has demonstrated exceptional leadership ability, and the training officers decided his efforts needed to be recognized. Men, join me in congratulating Fearsithe!"

"Huzzah! Huzzah!" the men shouted.

Two of our men from Williamsport, Doug Fessler and Rick Gordon, were awarded expert marksmanship badges as well. That rarely happened during the middle of training, but their rifle skills were so remarkable that they were to receive additional training for an elite role. I chuckled a little at the irony—neither man had ever shot a rifle prior to basic training. Rob and I quickly decided that, despite where we might end up, we always wanted Doug and Rick close by!

Our final day of basic training arrived on April 2 and began with an earlier than normal wake-up call. We were to engage in a simulated combat scenario. Our squad huddled together, smearing our faces with camouflage paint as our hearts raced with anticipation. We knew this exercise would test our training and teamwork. Sergeant O'Reilly spelled out the situation.

"The scenario takes place within a war-torn village in Poland, deep within the heart of enemy territory. Intelligence informed us the residents are about to be transported to one of the newly constructed extermination camps. It is your mission to neutralize the threat under the cover of early morning darkness and rescue the residents of the village. Corporal Fearsithe will lead the mission with PFC Smith as his second in command."

The sergeant concluded with a final briefing, emphasizing the importance of communication and situational awareness. Time was of the essence, and it would be light in ninety minutes. Three trucks transported us to the edge of the "village" on a rarely visited section of the fort.

I led the platoon to dense underbrush at the edge of the village where we would not be spotted. I deployed Rob with Fessler and Schrader as a reconnaissance team in the city.

Ten minutes later, my radio crackled with updates from our reconnaissance team as they monitored the enemy's movements. The tension was palpable as the remainder of the platoon and I carefully approached the village, our senses on high alert.

Suddenly, the silence was shattered by a burst of gunfire from a German outpost. We hit the ground and returned fire, muzzle flashes illuminating our faces in a surreal dance of light and shadow.

I ordered the platoon to split into two teams so we could flank the enemy. I put Private Gordon in charge of the second team. Bullets whizzed overhead, and the acrid smell of gunpowder hung in the air. It was chaos, but we held our positions, communicating with pre-arranged hand signals and whispered commands.

My heart pounded as we advanced through the village, taking cover behind crumbling walls and overturned carts. The enemy was determined, and every inch of ground was contested. It felt like an eternity, but in reality, it was only minutes before we had them cornered.

With precise coordination, we launched M16 smoke grenades to obscure their vision. As the thick, white smoke billowed around us, we closed in, our weapons at the ready. The enemy had no choice but to surrender.

We secured the remaining enemy combatants, bound their hands with rope, and freed the imprisoned villagers. We had successfully completed our mission; we immediately felt a sense of relief and accomplishment. The simulated combat had tested our mettle, but it had also reinforced the bonds of brotherhood. We were confident that, if called upon, we would face a real combat scenario as a well-trained, cohesive unit.

Later that afternoon, we gathered in formation on the parade grounds in our dress uniforms for final inspection. It was quite a different picture from the day of our arrival. Sergeant O'Reilly had painstakingly instilled within each one of us a great sense of detail.

We proudly passed in review before the officers and guests attending. Only a few men, who came from cities nearby, had family members in the stands. The rest of us discouraged our families from making the long journey.

Every man received some type of award, and most received more than one. Donny received the "Most Improved Recruit" award as expected, and a loud cheer went up from his fellow recruits. Jack Schrader was presented the "Outstanding Soldier Award" for exceptional dedication and discipline. Rob accepted the "Company Commander's Award" in recognition of his outstanding ability to lead, manage, and ensure the well-being of the men.

I was humbled to receive the "Distinguished Leadership Award" for exceptional leadership, effective team management, and contributing to the overall success of our unit. I later thanked the rest of our squad for making me look so good!

The other men in our platoon would be heading out the next morning for Camp Blanding, located outside of Starke, Florida, to join the First Battalion of the Eighteenth Regiment of the First Infantry Division. Lights out was delayed two hours that night so we could spend the evening celebrating together. We realized it might be the last time we had something to cheer about for a long time. I was amazed at how close we had all become in thirteen short weeks—and I would miss my brothers.

But the greatest honor that day came from Sergeant O'Reilly. He approached me during our celebration and quietly told me, "Corporal Fearsithe, in a few weeks, after you complete OCS, I will be saluting you and calling you 'sir' because of your rank. However, this evening, I salute you as a fellow non-commissioned officer in recognition of your outstanding performance here at training. There is no doubt you will make us proud, no matter where you end up serving."

"Thank you, sergeant," I replied, "for the investment you have made in my life. I won't forget it. And I promise, I will not let you down!"

The salutes we exchanged were the most earnest I ever exchanged with a superior—and there was no question in my mind that Sergeant O'Reilly was my superior . . . completely!

The following morning at 0800, after saying farewell to our platoon, Rob and I made our way to the Third Student Training Regiment on the other side of the base to report for Officer Candidate School Class Number 27. Since we were same-day transfers from basic training, we were able to skip much of the new arrivals process.

Our request to room together had been granted, and the duty sergeant directed us to the newly constructed hutment area east of Eighth Division and Woods Roads so we could stow our gear prior to orientation and briefing at 1000 hours. As it turned out, we would be billeting with two other men in one of the semi-cylindrical Quonset huts fabricated from corrugated metal. The Army was rapidly erecting these huts to accommo-date the growing influx of candidates.

When Rob and I arrived at our hut, we were surprised to find two colored men in uniform staring back at us. We hadn't seen any Negro soldiers on base since our arrival in January, so we were caught off guard. Once I got over my initial shock, I was dumbfounded to discover I knew one of the men, the stripes on his sleeve indicating that he, too, was a corporal.

"Larnell, is that you?"

"Yes, it is, Corporal Fearsithe," he replied with a grin. "And I expect I was the last person you thought you would see when you walked through that door. By the way, this here is PFC Frank Mack."

"It is a pleasure to meet you, private," I responded as I extended my hand. "I'm Corporal Bobby Fearsithe and this is PFC Rob Smith."

Frank shook my hand and said, "It is a pleasure to meet you both. Corporal Williams has told me a little bit about the two of you." Rob stepped forward and hesitantly shook both men's hands.

"Larnell, it seems you already knew you and Frank would be rooming with us, even though we had no idea," I said. "How is that?"

"We found out when we arrived this morning from Camp Lee," Larnell replied. "The two of us have been selected to be part of an experiment. We are the initial test case to determine whether white people and Negroes can be integrated during officer training. Apparently, Frank and I scored the highest among all the colored candidates, so we were selected.

"When they discovered you, Rob, and I were from Williamsport, they must have presumed we knew one another. So now you two are part of the experiment as well. By the way, Frank here is a fellow Pennsylvanian. He's from Philadelphia."

We stood there staring at each other for a few minutes, allowing this new information to sink in. Rob and I had anticipated our training would be challenging, but we never expected our performance would be subjected to the scrutiny of top brass in Washington.

"It's like we're going to be living in a fishbowl for the next three months," I commented to no one in particular.

"Actually, corporal," Larnell interjected, "you're about to discover what it's like to swim in our fishbowl. Orientation starts in fifteen minutes. We need to get going."

∼

5

FRIDAY MORNING, APRIL 3 – SATURDAY, JUNE 27, 1942

~

*T*here were two hundred men in our cohort, and we could feel the eyes of one hundred ninety-six of them, together with every officer in the room, pressing in on us as Colonel Robert H. Lord, the commanding officer of our OCS, began our orientation. During the course of his remarks, the colonel made a subtle reference to "the experiment in racial integration being conducted as a part of our class." All eyes focused on Larnell and Frank once more.

Colonel Lord explained that one of the many challenges of rapidly mobilizing and deploying our Army in this war was training a sufficient number of new officers.

"Up until now, we have been training eight classes simultaneously," he told the 200 candidates in our outfit. "We must now schedule almost 50 different classes to receive instruction simultaneously.

"This means ensuring the same terrain, troops, transportation, instructors, or equipment is not required by different classes at the same time. As you can imagine, the logistics of coordinating this gigantic puzzle has taken a great deal of planning and effort.

"You men are being trained as leaders who will navigate the many challenges still in our path to defeating our enemies in Europe, Africa, and Asia. I am confident you will rise to the occasion and reflect the high standards the world has come to expect from the United States Army. Not to mention, you will be bringing honor to your country and to your families."

Colonel Lord then called on Lt. Colonel George Helms, the assistant commandant, to outline our schedule for the next three days—considered the "processing cycle."

"When I dismiss you in a few minutes," Colonel Helms began, "each of you will begin the processing cycle by completing the forms needed for your OCS file, including a written autobiography. Your autobiography will be compared to your other records, and any discrepancies will need to be investigated and corrected before you proceed further."

I noticed the colonel looking directly at Larnell and Frank as he made his last point. After a brief pause for effect, he resumed.

"Tomorrow morning, each of you will be given a thorough medical and dental examination, even if you have just arrived here from basic training." This time he gazed right at Rob and me.

"You must pass those examinations before you are considered fully enrolled as a candidate. In the afternoon, identification photographs will be taken, and a provisional roster of this Officer Candidate Class will be posted.

. . .

"On the third day of the processing cycle, you will each complete an academic aptitude test. This measures your relative educational level and academic promise—regardless of whether your knowledge was acquired through schooling or through experience."

Again, the colonel stopped and looked directly at Larnell and Frank before proceeding.

"If you satisfactorily complete all those steps, you will be a fully enrolled student in OCS Class 27. One of the men standing behind me will serve as your tactical training officer."

He then introduced Chief Warrant Officers Winters, Meyer, Stull, and Weimer.

"On Monday morning," he continued, "those of you who are still here will be divided into four platoons. Each platoon will be under the supervision of one of these tactical training officers.

"With the exception of your scheduled formal instruction, which will be the responsibility of the academic department, your tactical training officer is charged with the responsibility for your discipline and development. He operates under the supervision of Colonel Lord and me.

"In addition, your training officers are responsible for instruction in voice and command training, physical training, and training in close order drill. With input from our academic faculty, these officers also are charged with judging your performance and determining whether you measure up to the standards of a U. S. Army combat platoon leader."

The colonel made a few more remarks before dismissing us to complete our paperwork. Before we left, he added, "Corporals Fearsithe and Williams, together with PFCs Mack and Smith, report to my office in five minutes for further briefing."

My roommates and I were not terribly surprised by this additional brief-ing. When we entered the room, we noticed two chairs positioned in front of the colonel's desk, behind which he was seated. The absence of two additional chairs clearly indicated we would be standing for this part of our orientation. The colonel wasted no time on pleasantries.

"Williams and Mack, I don't have to tell you that many of the men in your cohort do not want you here. And they aren't alone. The same holds true for most of the officers and instructors of this camp. The Army's segrega-tion of soldiers is based on prevailing public sentiment against mixing the races in the intimate association of military life. More to the point, military tradition has supported segregated units within the Army since 1863.

"Many of us believe that social integration will never be embraced by either race; therefore, why should we distract our fighting men with an unnecessary burden? Besides, it is placing too much responsibility on a race that has shown no initiative in battle. But our commander-in-chief has decided that since the enlistment of Negroes has increased significantly, we must ramp up our ability to train colored officers.

"As you men know, you are the initial experiment to determine whether whites and coloreds can, in fact, train together—academically, physically, and socially.

"Fearsithe and Smith, you were chosen for this trial because we believed the two of you had some prior acquaintance with Williams. I must warn you both that your association with these men, and your agreement to participate in this social experiment, will not be seen favorably by most of your fellow students. You will be subjected to more pressure and scrutiny than any of your counterparts.

"So, men, I must ask if any of you would prefer not to take part in this experiment. Colonel Lord and I do not want you to participate unwillingly. If that is the case, now is the time for you to speak up."

Larnell was the first to reply.

"Colonel Helms, PFC Mack and I volunteered to participate in this trial. We signed up to be a part of this man's Army to defend our nation—white and colored—against the forces of tyranny. We want the best training we can get to lead our men—white or colored—and I figure the best training is here at Fort Benning. I understand we will all have to learn how to do this together, but I figure all of us have two common enemies—Adolf Hitler and Emperor Hirohito—and we can set aside any racial differences in order to defeat them."

"Colonel," I began, "I've known of Corporal Williams for several years, but I've not known him well—let alone enough to call us friends. But I've never even thought about why we didn't know each other. However, hearing him now, I can tell you I want the same thing he wants. I want to see our enemies defeated. We can do that better together than we can apart. So I am in favor of learning how to do just that. And if others can learn from our mistakes and successes, I think it's worth doing. So, you can count me in as well, sir!"

"Like Corporal Williams said," PFC Mack spoke up, "we already volunteered for this. We knew it wouldn't be a cakewalk, sir. But like he said, if there was ever something worth doing, it's this. You can count me in, too, sir!"

Everyone in the room turned and faced Rob.

"Colonel, I'd be lying to you and to these men if I didn't confess I have some misgivings," he said. "But, truth be told, I didn't expect to get into this particular OSC class. And yet, I did. Now I can't help but wonder if it was so I could be part of this experiment.

"I don't know these two men well, but I know if we are called to sacrifice for our country, the blood we shed will be the same color regardless of the color of our skin. So, if it's all the same to you, Colonel, I'd like to know we all got the best training possible. And I think that's what this is all about. So you can most definitely count me in!"

The colonel hesitated for a moment. "Men, I commend your dedication to your country, but you must understand that not everyone will share your sentiment and overlook the color of your skin. But I would say if I had to choose the four men to take part in this experiment, you four would be the ones. Good luck! You're dismissed!"

We saluted the colonel and left his office more committed to the task than ever. Over the next few days, we focused on completing the necessary steps of our processing cycle—the countless forms, the exhaustive autobiography, and the stem-to-stern cattle prodding the Army calls a medical and dental examination.

On Sunday morning, we completed the final part of the checklist—our academic aptitude test. It might have been my imagination, but I felt as if every eye on the base was watching and hoping Larnell and Frank would wash out.

The irony was not lost on the four of us that the Army's initial integration experiment was taking place on a fort named after a Confederate general. Of course, then again, the camp where Larnell and Frank had received their basic training was named after General Robert E. Lee. We decided the Army would need to make a lot of changes, including renaming their camps, if they hoped to bring the races together on equal footing.

The chasm between us four and the other men was most noticeable in the mess hall. Though the seating was calculated to accommodate the exact number of candidates and supervising officers, there were always empty chairs at our table.

Chief Warrant Officer Winters summoned me Sunday afternoon for my intake interview. He was a career soldier in his early fifties, with thinning gray hair and average height, and he was in excellent physical condition. I later learned he had enlisted in the Army two years before the U.S. entered World War I and had remained ever since.

The purpose of the interview was to draw out the facts of a candidate's life that might affect his work at the school or his leadership abilities. We had been told that the tactical officer would make every effort to know each candidate intimately in order to give an accurate assessment. Those interviews would then be repeated during the candidate's training to monitor his accomplishments.

After our exchange of salutes, Chief Winters directed me to sit in the metal chair in front of his desk. A folder was opened in front of him, apparently containing my intake records. I quickly realized this interview would be as cool and stark as the room in which we were seated.

"Corporal Fearsithe, I have reviewed your records," he began, "and I must say I am quite impressed with what I see. But I would expect no less from Captain Gene Fearsithe's son."

"Do you know my father, chief?" I asked.

"Only by reputation. There is no question he made an important contribution to our efforts in the First World War. He set a high bar for you."

Changing the subject, he continued. "I understand you and PFC Smith did not volunteer to take part in this integration experiment but rather were chosen for the assignment. How does that make you feel, corporal?"

"I received it like any other order a commanding officer would give me," I replied. "I don't get to pick and choose which orders I'm going to accept. My responsibility is to carry out those orders to the best of my ability."

"Yes, I know you understand the meaning of the chain of command," the chief responded. "But I want to know how it makes you feel."

"Colonel Helms actually gave us an opportunity to turn down the assignment. But I told him I want to see our enemies defeated, and I believe coloreds and whites can do that better working together than apart. So I am in favor of learning how to do that the best we can. And if others can learn from our mistakes and successes, I think it's worth doing."

"What do you think of Corporal Williams and PFC Mack?" the chief pressed.

"I really haven't known them long, chief," I replied. "But from what I've seen so far, they seem like good men who love their country and are willing to lay down their lives for freedom. That makes them okay in my book."

"How do you feel about sharing a barracks with Negroes?"

"Probably no different than they feel about sharing a barracks with white men."

"So you don't have any reservations about this experiment?" the chief probed.

"To be perfectly honest, I do have one reservation. I would feel much better if everyone stopped making such a big deal about it. The Declaration of Independence says, 'All men are created equal' and are 'endowed by their Creator with certain unalienable Rights.' We fought a Civil War not that long ago over that very issue. I think it's time we stopped refighting that war every day and lived like we really believe this founding document. That's what I think, chief. And if this experiment can help us move closer to living that way, I'm all for it!"

I walked away from that conference not really knowing if Chief Winters was in favor of the experiment or not; he had remained noncommittal. But our time together made me even more determined to make this trial a success. It was time this Army—and this country—moved past this segregation business!

Larnell, Frank, and Rob had their conferences with the chief that afternoon too. And each of them had pretty much the same conversation, except the chief pressed Larnell and Frank even harder about resigning from the experiment. But the result was that all of us walked away even more committed. I'd like to think that was his desired outcome … but I must confess, I'm not really sure.

Platoon assignments were posted Monday morning, and our four names were part of Alpha Platoon's roster under the supervision of Chief Warrant Officer Winters.

For the next thirteen weeks, we went through vigorous training in the proper use and care of weapons, as well as tactics, discipline, and administration. I found it interesting that out of the 534 hours of scheduled instruction, only four hours was designated to the subject of leadership. But I quickly realized leadership was embedded in everything we were being taught.

My roommates and I also learned lessons that were not listed in the OCS syllabus. Rob and I learned how to live under the oppression of racism and bigotry. Larnell and Frank entered into OCS having lived under that oppression all of their lives—and they taught us how to respond from their lifetime of learning. We were the newcomers, and even though we felt its effects, we knew our experience was nothing in comparison to theirs.

However, the four of us never allowed the words, threats, and, in a few instances, actions cause us to waver from our goal. By the last four weeks of OCS, we began to sense a degree of respect—or at least a lessening of animosity—from the other candidates as well as the supervising officers.

I'm sure part of it was due to our high-scoring performances and accomplishments in exercises and competitions. But I also believe our class realized we truly were a band of brothers. It didn't matter where you came from, how much money you had, or even the color of your skin.

In his graduation address to us, Colonel Lord declared, "The world of the future will owe a debt of gratitude to you—the officers of today. You will encounter enemies unlike any who have come before, using weaponry and strategies heretofore unimagined. And you will overcome them with the strength, determination, and dedication you have proven during your time here

"You leave this place owing a debt to yesterday's officers. It was their vision and persistence in overcoming their enemies that has paved the way for the excellent training you have received. Because of their foresight, you are leaving this place better prepared than they were to tackle any and every challenge you will encounter.

"Now it is up to you to pay forward the investment they have made in you! Just as you have benefitted from the knowledge of their mistakes and achievements, learn from your own. Build an even better pathway into the future. Make them proud!"

∼

6

SUNDAY, JUNE 28, 1942 – TUESDAY, MAY 11, 1943

∼

The following morning our entire class—all of us now holding the rank of Second Lieutenant—headed out to meet up with the units to which we had been assigned. That meant Rob and I were headed to Camp Blanding to join our battalion in the First Infantry Division; Larnell and Frank were going back to Camp Lee to join the Ninety-Second Infantry Division.

"I'm not sure what I expected when Rob and I encountered you two that first day," I said to Larnell and Frank, looking each man in the eye. "But I'm a better soldier—and a better man—because of what we have been through together. I hope we've smoothed the path for those who come behind us. You are both mighty fine officers, and I would count it a privilege to serve under either one of you.

"But more importantly to me, you are mighty fine men. You've taught me when to hold my peace and when to speak up. You've shown me when to stand my ground and when to leave a matter alone. And you've shown me there's a whole lot more to a man than the color of his skin."

"Bobby, I think I can speak for Frank, too, when I say you and Rob have shown us that integration is possible," Larnell replied. "We not only learned to acknowledge one another, but we also learned to respect and value one another. So, besides learning to defeat the threats to our freedom outside our country, maybe this war will teach us how to defeat the threats of racial discrimination within our country. I know it will if more men are willing to explore what the four of us have learned here."

Just then our transport arrived. Rob and I shook their hands as I said, "Larnell and Frank, I don't know when—or even if—we'll see each other again. Who knows, we may find ourselves fighting side by side when we get to Europe. But whenever and however, watch out for each other. Give the enemy hell—and may God go with you."

Eight hours later, Rob and I arrived at Camp Blanding, which was about a third the size of Fort Benning. It was also a much newer facility, having been built only three years earlier. It was named after General Albert Blanding, who had distinguished himself in the First War as well as in contributions to military preparedness following the war.

We set out to locate our infantry battalion which was a part of the First Division. Major General Terry Allen was in command of the division. He was a decorated First War veteran who had commanded a battalion at the age of thirty and been wounded in battle twice.

The First Division, known as "Red One Division" or "Fighting First," as we preferred to be called, had made quite a name for itself in the First War. It had been the first division to arrive in France, it also was the first to see action at the front, the first U.S. division to fire on the enemy, to raid, and to suffer casualties.

The Eighteenth Regiment within the First Division was under the command of Colonel Frank Greer. We were looking for Captain Henry Learnard, who commanded the First Battalion within that regiment. We eventually caught up with him as he was overseeing the men under his command as they were going through their paces on the obstacle course. As it turned out, the men were from my platoon.

"Gentlemen, your reputations precede you," the captain told us. "These men who went through basic training with you speak very highly of your leadership. Also, Colonel Helms wrote me commending you both for the excellent manner in which you conducted yourselves in the racial integration experiment at OCS.

"As a matter of fact, Lieutenant Fearsithe, both he and Colonel Lord recommended you for promotion to First Lieutenant. That is very timely for me, as your orders are to take over the leadership of this platoon, Platoon Alpha. I knew I would be seeing you today so I placed your silver bar in my pocket. Allow me to remove your gold bar and replace it with this one."

The captain saluted me as he said, "Congratulations, First Lieutenant Fearsithe, on this well-earned promotion. I look forward to seeing your leadership abilities in person as you command this platoon.

"And Lieutenant Smith, welcome to the First Battalion," he added as he shook Rob's hand. "I am placing you in Platoon Alpha as Lieutenant Fearsithe's second in command. I trust that will be satisfactory for you."

"Yes, sir," Rob replied with a sharp salute.

Once the men completed the obstacle course, the captain called the platoon to attention and introduced Rob and me as their new commanding officers.

"I know you men already know the lieutenants and will support them as they transition into their new positions," he said. "I fully expect this platoon to be the tip of the spear of the First Division when we enter into the fray. So look sharp, get prepared, and make us proud! Dismissed!"

After they were dismissed, the men surrounded us and gave us a grand welcome. Donny was the first to step up and greet us. He gave me a sharp salute and said, "Welcome, Lieutenant Fearsithe. We have been looking forward to your arrival!"

I could tell he had grown as a leader in the three months since I last saw him, and I could see the respect the platoon had for him as well. He was by no means the nervous wallflower who had shown up at Fort Benning just six months earlier.

Right behind Donny was Jack Schrader, who gave me a snappy salute followed quickly by a firm handshake. "We've missed you guys, Lieutenant," he declared. He, too, had obviously become even more of a leader among this group. I knew I would need to initiate action soon to formally recognize the roles of these two.

The men led us to the barracks so we could store our duffel bags before we headed to the mess hall. We spent the evening swapping stories about everything that had happened since we last saw one another.

After an additional month's training, there was no question that our regiment was as prepared for deployment as possible; we were all ready to see action. Though we knew our months of training served an important purpose, we were aware our most important lessons would be learned on the battlefield.

We received our orders on August 7. Colonel Greer assembled the regiment and announced, "Tomorrow morning at 0700, buses will depart for Newport News, Virginia, where we will board a naval transport bound for Southampton, England. Upon arrival, we will make our way 100 miles inland to Tewkesbury, England, where a large camp has recently been constructed for our forces. Our regiment will be among the first U.S. forces to place their feet on European soil. May God go before us!"

During our journey across the Atlantic, our officers cautioned us not to spend our money too freely in Britain. This was partly for fear of destabilizing the value of the British currency, as well as to avoid fueling the widespread apprehension in Britain that American troops were "oversexed, overpaid, and over here."

Ironically, within two months of our arrival, the local newspaper became less concerned about Brits sufficiently welcoming American soldiers and more preoccupied with concerns that some locals were being too friendly! On October 24, the Tewkesbury Register and Gazette published this article:

Girls Who Hang Round Camps

The Gloucestershire Federation of Women's Institutes has passed a resolution that the time has come to increase the number of women police in the county in response to the increasing number of young girls who have begun to hang around the American Army camp at night.

The proposer, a Mrs. Vernon, believes that increased supervision will deter them, blaming the girls and their parents for this situation, but not the soldiers themselves. The applause given in response to this proposal suggests that there is considerable goodwill felt towards the American soldiers.[1]

In early November we returned to the English coast to board a transport ship that was part of a large convoy headed for the North African coastline. At 0016 hours on November 8, we went ashore at Oran, Algeria, as the first U.S. Army infantry units to engage in combat against Axis forces. The offensive, called "Operation Torch," was the largest, most complex, and riskiest military operation yet mounted in the war. It was the first major Allied amphibious assault, and scuttlebutt was that it had been hastily planned and patched together. But my platoon and I were grateful to finally be engaging in the fight. It had taken us almost a year to get there.

The full campaign involved about 65,000 troops who landed at Casablanca and Algiers, in addition to Oran, all on the French North African coast. The Germans had a limited presence in the area at the time, so we expected to primarily encounter Vichy French forces. We met minimal opposition on the beaches despite mistimed landings caused by poor planning.

The disembarkation and offloading went smoothly until two of our escort vessels—the HMS Walney and the HMS Hartland—were fired upon and reduced to flaming hulks by a French sloop and crossfire from other vessels. Both crafts sank and 234 officers and crew were lost.

On land, however, we quickly captured the shore battery with minimal casualties. We gained ground throughout the day as the fighting continued. I was proud of my men's performance and the way they watched out for one another. And I was relieved that no one in our platoon was injured or lost. By the end of the day, we had captured Oran with the help of a British tank division; within three days the other two cities had also been captured.

It was on that first campaign I learned that victory on the battlefield often comes by providence—not necessarily as a result of good planning. A fortuitous event worked to our advantage during those initial days. Admiral Jean François Darlan, commander in chief of Vichy forces, happened to be in Algiers visiting his sick son. During planning, U.S. commanders had chosen General Henri Giraud—who had escaped from German captivity in France—to assume local control as we made our advance.

But when it became clear he lacked the authority to establish it, our superiors turned to Admiral Darlan. Having been taken into protective custody, the wily admiral was persuaded by the strength of our Allied force to change sides. He broke with the odious Vichy regime, and an armistice was signed on November 11. The armistice enabled our Allied forces to swiftly take control of coastal Morocco and Algeria.

Though I believe it was unintentional on the part of our U.S. generals—including General Dwight Eisenhower, the supreme commander of the Allied forces in the Mediterranean—the deployment of our newly trained U.S. forces on the periphery of the Nazi empire proved to be a sound strategy. It provided our inexperienced Army with invaluable combat experience.

For example, it highlighted our need for better planning, less recklessness, and much greater coordination—the lack of which had resulted in a number of setbacks. But we learned those hard lessons quickly, and foundations were laid in North Africa to strengthen our American force. "Operation Torch" was a proving ground on which generals and privates alike learned the harsh facts of warfare before facing German General Erwin Rommel's acclaimed Afrika Korps and the rest of the battle-seasoned Wehrmacht.

The British and American armies made steady advances from east and west, but by mid-November, 1,000 German troops were arriving each day in northern Tunisia. That number was a sobering thought for everyone in my platoon.

The first enemy units arriving from Vichy on November 16 were the Fifth Panzer Army under the command of Hermann Göring. They were immediately deployed westward to hold the line of the eastern Atlas Mountains against our advancing forces—which included our platoon. Göring's arrival stalled our advance on the strategic Tunisian city of Bizerte.

His impenetrable wall of tanks, combined with an onslaught of unseasonal inclement weather, kept us pinned down for weeks. Mud and rain delayed our reinforcements coming from Algiers, 500 miles to the west. 1942 ended with our Allied and the Axis forces in a stalemate.

By February 18, we were engaged by the enemy at Kasserine Pass, a two-mile-wide gap in the Grand Dorsal chain of the Atlas Mountains. The battle proved to be my baptism by fire. The pass, with its rocky cliffs and winding roads, had seemed like a natural fortress where we could hold our position, but it quickly turned into a deadly trap.

The initial German assault was swift and relentless. Our unit was pinned down under a barrage of heavy artillery fire with enemy tanks advancing from all directions. The confusion was overwhelming, and the air was thick with the stench of smoke and fear.

I desperately tried to maintain command amid the pandemonium, shouting orders to my men over the din of battle. But it felt like a losing battle, with each passing moment bringing us closer to the brink of defeat.

"Keep your heads down!" I shouted. "We must hold this position at all costs!"

"Sir, they're coming at us from all sides!" Donny shouted back. "We can't hold them off much longer!"

"I know it's tough, but we can't give up now!" I replied. "We've got to dig in deeper and fight harder!"

Rob made his way over to me and quietly asked, "What's the plan, Lieutenant? We're outnumbered and outgunned!"

"We hold this ground until reinforcements arrive," I answered. "And if they don't, we fight until the last breath in our bodies!"

"But Bobby, it feels like we're fighting a losing battle!" Rob responded.

"We might be," I replied, "but we'll make every moment count! We owe it to those who've fallen before us and to those who'll come after us. We fight for them, for our families, for our country!"

Jack, who had apparently overheard our conversation, asked, "What if we don't make it, Lieutenant?"

"Then we'll make sure they remember us!" I declared loud enough for everyone to hear. "We'll make them pay for every inch they take from us!"

"Sir, they're advancing!" Rick Gordon called out.

"Then we make our stand here and now!" I shouted. "Hold the line, men! Hold the line!"

Despite the overwhelming odds, the resilience and determination of my men was awe-inspiring. We fought tooth and nail, refusing to yield an inch of ground to the Germans. But for every step forward we took, it seemed like the enemy pushed us two steps back.

Finally, the First Armored Division arrived, bringing with it a glimmer of hope to our platoon. The presence of those tanks, under the command of General George Patton, infused our entire regiment with renewed energy and determination, rallying us for one final push against the enemy. And though the battle was far from over, the arrival of those tanks changed the balance of power and gave us the ability to press forward.

That was the turning point of the Tunisian Campaign. But it wasn't without cost. Several of my men were wounded that day, and Private

Doug Fessler, one of my fellow Williamsporters, lost his life. He was the first … but I feared he wouldn't be the last before this war was over.

When I think back on those dark days at Kasserine Pass, I am filled with a mix of pride and sorrow: pride for the bravery and sacrifice of my fellow soldiers, and sorrow for the lives lost in the crucible of war. It was a trial by fire that tested us to the core, but it was also a testament to the indomitable spirit of the American soldier.

Once we were through the pass, we encountered the enemy again at El Guettar, Béja, and Mateur on our way to Tunis. The rugged terrain and scorching Tunisian sun added to the already daunting challenges of combat. We advanced cautiously, mindful of the enemy's determination and the potential for ambushes around every corner.

The closer we got to Tunis, the fiercer the fighting became. Urban warfare presented its own set of challenges as we navigated through narrow streets and alleyways, often coming face to face with entrenched Axis defenders.

Despite the upheaval and uncertainty of battle, the camaraderie among the men in our regiment was unwavering. We relied on each other for support and encouragement, drawing strength from our shared determination to see the mission through to the end.

On the morning of May 7, as we entered the city of Tunis, the roar of artillery shells and the crackle of small arms fire echoed through the streets. Every step brought us closer to victory, but it also exacted a heavy price as we witnessed the sacrifices of our comrades.

Finally, after days of intense fighting, the Axis defenses crumbled under the weight of our relentless assault—and the enemy was forced to surrender. It was a bittersweet victory, tempered by the realization of the toll it had taken on both sides.

As we surveyed the ruins of Tunis, I was proud of what our platoon had accomplished. We had overcome seemingly insurmountable odds to achieve our objective, and in doing so, we had played a crucial role in turning the tide of the war in North Africa.

The Allied occupation of the entire North African coast would now open the Mediterranean to Allied shipping, allowing our forces to maintain supplies around the circuitous route via the Cape of Good Hope.

[1]   From Tewkesbury Museum – "Memories of Ashchurch: The Americans"

https://www.tewkesburymuseum.org/the-collection/the-archive-collection/memories-of-ashchurch/the-americans/

7

WEDNESDAY, MAY 12 – WEDNESDAY, AUGUST 18, 1943

❧

*I*n recognition of their heroic performance at Kasserine Pass, I put through recommendations for Donny Busey to be promoted from PFC to corporal and Rob Smith from second lieutenant to first lieutenant. Those commendations were immediately approved, as was Major Learnard's recommendation that I be promoted to captain.

Over the next several weeks, our regimental assignment was to secure the occupation of the North African coast. I think we were all grateful for the calmer duty after the intensity of the previous six months. We received orders the first week of July to join the launch of Operation Husky. Our battalion boarded a transport ship in Tunisia on July 9 and arrived at our assembly area off the southern coast of Sicily at 2200 hours that same day.

We watched as the initial troops landed on the beaches of Gela under the cover of darkness. They were met by small arms fire from Italian defenders. The plan was to capture the pier so it could be used for offloading our tank landing ships, or LSTs, as they were otherwise called. But the Italian defenders quickly destroyed the pier before it could be secured.

"Captain, since the pier is demolished, what's our next move?" one of the men in my platoon asked.

"Well, we adapt and work around it. The Army engineers will be devising a solution even as we speak. Our priority will shift to clearing the mines so our LSTs can start offloading troops and equipment. It's going to be a tough job, but these men have been trained in what to do. And we need to trust their training."

After sunrise, the minesweepers began operations to clear mines near the beach for the LSTs. However, a number of mine detectors proved unreliable after their exposure to salt water during the landing. That slowed progress, and it was 1212 hours before the first path was cleared.

By that time, we learned the Axis forces were being reinforced by Italian artillery and German bombers. Our troops had limited support from Allied aircraft and the few tanks that had successfully landed. Our regiment was not called to go ashore until later that day, so we watched helplessly as the landings continued. Finally at 1700 hours we were called up.

The late afternoon sun bore down as our landing craft approached the shore. No one spoke as we braced ourselves for what lay ahead. As the ramp dropped, I gave my men a reassuring nod.

The deafening roar of artillery and small arms fire engulfed us as we stepped onto the blood-soaked sand. Havoc reigned as we scrambled for cover, the beach littered with the bodies of soldiers who had preceded us. I barked orders to my men, trying to maintain some semblance of order amid the cacophony of war.

Our objective was clear—push inland and secure vital positions to establish a foothold on the island. But that was far more daunting than any briefing could convey. The enemy, dug in deep and determined to hold their ground, fought ferociously, contesting every inch of territory.

Gunfire from our support ships enabled us to hold the beach as darkness fell. Troops who had preceded us in an attempt to advance on the town were now falling back to our position.

The next morning, every man on the beach—including naval yeomen, electricians, carpenters, and intelligence and supply officers of the Advanced Naval Base Group—was hastily armed and placed on a firing line along the dunes.

"Hold the line, men, hold the line!" I shouted emphatically. "Rick and Jack, get to that high point on the dune and put your sharp-shooter training to good use! Make sure the engineers are able to keep working!"

The Army engineers continued their work to make a way for the Allied tanks to come ashore. Gunfire support from the ships resumed at 0915.

By midday, the engineering solutions combined with further minesweeping efforts provided a path for the landing of Allied tanks. By dawn the following morning, 90 percent of our Allied convoy was unloaded.

I sent out Rodriguez and Wilson to scout out our best approach into the town of Gela. They soon returned with a less than optimistic report. Rob and I weighed the options they had given us as we discussed the best route for our men to advance from the beach into the town. What awaited us was a landscape that morphed into a nightmarish battleground.

"Holy mackerel!" Rob muttered as we surveyed buildings lying in ruins and streets littered with rubble and debris. Every step forward felt like a gamble with death as we cautiously scouted for the enemy.

Yet, our platoon pressed on, relying on our training and our instinct. The sound of gunfire and explosions became a symphony of war, a constant reminder of the stakes at hand.

Eventually, the tide began to turn in our favor. Inch by inch, we gained ground in Gela and obtained key objectives.

"Keep pushing the enemy back, men!" I commanded as we secured the Ponte Olivo airfield on the outskirts of town. Now we could provide ground support for air operations against German and Italian forces.

Despite our triumphs, the cost was undeniable. Faces of fallen comrades haunted me, a sobering reminder of the sacrifices made in the name of freedom. As the dust settled and the echoes of battle faded, I wondered what lay ahead in this war-torn land.

I looked into the faces of my men and saw their exhaustion. "Men, I'm proud of each and every one of you, and the way you have performed to get us this far. Your actions are a testament to your courage and determination. As we take a moment to regroup, I want you to know that whatever is up ahead, I am confident we will prevail. Because I know you men, and I wouldn't want to be here with anyone else!"

Three weeks later on August 7, the morning sun cast long shadows across the rugged terrain as our battalion gathered for what we knew would be a defining moment in the Sicilian Campaign. Mount Pellegrino loomed ominously in the distance. Our mission was simple yet daunting—to capture the heights and provide our artillery with a clear line of sight to the defenses surrounding the strategic city of Troina.

Anticipation mingled with a sense of urgency as we advanced toward the base of the mountain. We were aware the enemy was entrenched on the slopes. Every step forward felt like a step closer to the jaws of death.

I noticed the men ahead of us had stopped for a short rest. I called out to the platoon to circle up.

"All right, listen up, everyone!" I declared. "We're approaching the base of Mount Pellegrino. Keep your heads down and stay alert. The enemy knows we're coming, so expect heavy resistance."

"Captain, what do you think our chances are of taking the mountain?" Private Rodriguez asked.

"Our orders are clear, Rodriguez. We don't have a choice. It's vital for our artillery to have a clear line of sight to the Troina defenses. We've trained for this, and we're going to give it everything we've got. So I think our chances are good."

One of the other men, Private Johnson, asked, "What's the plan once we reach the summit, sir?"

"We'll dig in and hold our ground. Expect counterattacks from the enemy, so be prepared to repel them at all costs."

"What if we encounter heavy resistance, sir?" Donny asked.

"We will push through it, corporal, just like we did at Gela. We can't afford to get bogged down. Remember your training, stay together, and watch each other's backs. We've faced tough odds before, and we've always come out on top."

"Captain, what if we don't make it?" Private Martinez asked quietly.

"We'll make it, Martinez. We have a job to do, and failure is not an option. You men are prepared for this! Trust in yourself and in the man to your left and the one to your right. And most importantly, trust God! He goes before us. We've got this."

"Sir, do you think the rest of the regiment will make it?" a fellow Williamsporter, Bill Martin, asked.

"They will, if we do our part, Martin. Our success here will pave the way for the rest of the regiment to advance. They're counting on each one of us to give it his all."

The men up ahead were back on the move, so I said, "Okay, let's move out. Keep your wits about you and stay focused. Mount Pellegrino awaits, and we're going to take it by storm!"

The steep climb up the ridge was arduous, testing our endurance and resolve. The enemy fought fiercely to hold their ground, raining down a barrage of mortar fire and machine gun bullets. Yet, we pressed upward, driven by a singular purpose—to seize control of the heights.

As we reached the summit, the men's exhaustion was fused with exhilaration as we took in the breathtaking panorama before us. But there was little time to savor the moment as we immediately set about fortifying our position and preparing for the inevitable counterattacks.

From our vantage point, we could see the Troina defenses stretched out before us like a web of steel and concrete. Our capture of the heights had provided our artillery with the advantage they needed, allowing them to pummel the enemy below.

But the battle was far from over. Throughout the day and into the night, our adversaries launched wave after wave of counterattacks in a desperate bid to dislodge us from our perch. Yet, my men repelled each assault with fierce determination.

As the sun dipped below the horizon and the stars emerged, we knew that victory was within our grasp. The capture of Mount Pellegrino had bolstered the morale of our troops and dealt a crippling blow to our foes' defenses.

With gunfire echoing in the distance, I stared into the flickering glow of the campfire that night with a sense of accomplishment. We had achieved our objective without losing a single soldier in my battalion. My men had fought bravely, and I could not have been prouder of them.

The defeat at Troina convinced the Germans to withdraw their troops from Sicily across the Strait of Messina. Their retreat scheme proved to be so successful that our Allied forces were unable to prevent their withdrawal or interfere with their transports. The narrow strait was protected by 120 heavy and 112 light anti-aircraft guns. The overlapping gunfire from both sides of the strait prevented our pilots from attacking.

The sun had barely risen when we received orders to push toward Messina and secure the city. Though the German forces had withdrawn, the Italian forces still remained—which meant the road ahead of us was dangerous. Our unit was tasked with leading the advance. As I addressed my men, I could see the fatigue, but also the courage, etched on their faces.

Treacherous terrain and a stubborn Italian resistance made our trek toward Messina difficult. The Italians fought fiercely to hold onto their last stronghold in Sicily. Artillery shells screamed overhead, and the crackle of small arms fire rang through the countryside as we marched forward.

The fighting intensified the closer we got to Messina. The streets became a chaotic battleground, littered with rubble and carnage. Our progress was slow and measured, every inch we gained coming at a heavy cost.

Like any other battle, strategic decisions had to be made on the fly, weighing risks and rewards in the heat of combat. The lives of my men hung in the balance with every command I issued, and the weight of responsibility bore down on me.

Enemy defenses began to crumble under the assault of our forces, and eventually Messina was ours. But the mood was dampened as we mourned the loss of our fallen brothers. Bill Martin was among our casualties that day, and Johnson and Rodriguez were both injured.

Even so, I took comfort knowing our victory would pave the way for the eventual liberation of Sicily and the triumph of freedom over tyranny.

8

THURSDAY, AUGUST 19, 1943 – SUNDAY, JUNE 11, 1944

⤳

*T*gathered my unit together early the next morning to go over details of our next objective.

"Men, we are to take control of the Strait of Messina that divides Sicily and Italy as we push into the Italian peninsula. The Germans still have control of the guns lining both sides of the strait. There is no likelihood we can dislodge them from their secure positions with an assault from the Sicily side; we need to attack from the Italian side. That means Allied forces will assault two coastal cities simultaneously—Calabria, directly across from Sicily, and our objective, the port of Salerno, further north on the western coast of Italy.

"Any questions?" I asked, as the group nodded their understanding. "No sir!" they replied in unison.

The amphibious attack on Calabria, named "Operation Baytown," was conducted by British and Canadian forces on September 3. American and British forces followed with an assault on the port of Salerno, named

"Operation Avalanche," on September 9. Our goal was to seize the port, cutting off resupply for the Axis forces and ensuring resupply for our troops. We would then cut across to the east coast of Italy, trapping our foes between us and those of Operation Baytown to the south.

Though our landings at Salerno were supposed to catch the enemy by surprise, that was not the case. Instead, our arrival was met by the enemy's chilling message in English through a loudspeaker on shore: "Come on in and give up. We have you covered."

I glanced at my men and was pleased to find nothing but readiness and determination on their faces. The enemy's taunts only fueled our resolve to push forward. We knew the mission's success depended on our breaking through the enemy's defenses and establishing a foothold on the shore.

Pandemonium best describes the scene on the beach as gunfire and explosions from the enemy's firmly entrenched artillery and machine-gun positions met with the response from our naval support. Fellow soldiers shouting orders mingled with cries from wounded and dying soldiers.

Every step forward was hard won, with each inch of ground gained representing a victory against overwhelming odds. Our success in taking the beach, however, came at the expense of heavy casualties. Several of my men were injured in the fray. But we continued to persevere in the weeks ahead, and by early October the whole of southern Italy was under Allied control.

The next stage for our Allied armies in the overall campaign to take control of the remainder of Italy was a grinding and attritional slog against skillful, determined and well-prepared defenses, made even more difficult by the rugged terrain and the severe weather conditions which favored the Axis defenses and hampered the advantages we possessed in mechanized equipment and air superiority.

We gained ground slowly. Our regiment enjoyed little rest, and the soldiers were exhausted. Our commanding officer, General Clark, was mindful of the toll exacted on his battle-weary troops. So, with Thanksgiving approaching, he arranged to have special rations airdropped to us in order to momentarily take our minds off the war and turn our thoughts toward happier times .

He even had makeshift tables setup in our encampments and for our platoons to rotate through for this special meal while the others kept watch against the enemy. A modest spread of rations was laid out before us, but at that moment it looked and tasted like a homemade Thanksgiving meal.

"All right boys," I said. "Gather round. I reckon it's time we gave thanks, just like we would back home."

"Captain, how about you say grace for us?" Rob suggested.

We took off our helmets, bowed our heads, and closed our eyes—something we hadn't been able to do before a meal since we landed at Salerno.

"Almighty and merciful God, on this day of Thanksgiving, amidst the trials and tribulations of war, we come before you with grateful hearts," I prayed. "Though we may be far from our loved ones and the comforts of home, we are grateful for the bond that unites us as brothers in arms.

"We thank You for the strength and courage You have bestowed upon us, guiding us through the darkest of days and giving us hope for the future. We appreciate the camaraderie that sustains us, lifting our spirits in times of despair and reminding us that we are never alone.

"As we gather around these humble tables, we give thanks for the food before us, knowing that even in times of scarcity, You provide for our needs. May this simple meal nourish our bodies and strengthen our resolve as we continue to serve our country with honor and dignity.

"We also remember those who are unable to be with us today—our comrades who have made the ultimate sacrifice in defense of freedom. May their memory be a source of inspiration and courage as we carry on their legacy.

"Lord, we ask for Your blessings upon our families back home, keeping them safe and comforted in our absence. Grant them strength and resilience as they await our return.

"Finally, we pray for peace in this troubled world, that nations may come together in harmony and goodwill, laying down their arms in pursuit of a brighter tomorrow.

"In your mercy, hear our prayers, O Lord, and bless this Thanksgiving Day with your grace and love. In Christ's name we pray."

The men lifted their heads, as together we said, "Amen."

"Thanks for that prayer, captain," Private Jackson said. "It reminds me of the prayer my granddaddy usually prays around our Thanksgiving table at home. Sure wish I could be back in Texas right now, sitting 'round the table with my folks, stuffing myself silly with Grandma's cornbread stuffing."

"Ah, cornbread stuffing sounds like heaven right about now," Private Aker added. "I'd give anything for a slice of pumpkin pie too."

"Yeah, and I miss hearing my abuelita's stories about how she celebrated

Thanksgiving back in Mexico," Private Martinez added. "The whole family would gather 'round and share what we were thankful for."

"I hear ya, Martinez," Jack Schrader replied. "Back in Williamsport, we'd have a big feast with all the trimmings. Mom's turkey was legendary, and Dad would always carve it up with a flourish."

"It sounds like we're all missing home a little extra today," I said, "as we should. But you know what? We may be far away from our families back home, but we're still a family right here. And we've got plenty to be thankful for, like each other and the fact that we're all still standing strong."

"Amen to that, captain," Rob added. "And hey, we may not have Mom's cooking or Grandma's stories, but we've got each other. And that's something worth celebrating."

Donny had been quiet since we sat down, but now he spoke up.

"You know what? You're right, Lieutenant Smith! We may be miles away from home, but we've still got a lot to be grateful for right here, right now. So let's dig in and enjoy this meal together."

Each platoon member raised his canteen cup in a makeshift toast before we dug into our rations. Despite the absence of home comforts, there was a sense of gratitude and community that filled the air as we celebrated Thanksgiving that day. And each man knew it was a moment—and a meal —he would never forget.

When our time was over, we gratefully took our time on watch so the next platoon could come take our place.

≈

It took until mid-January 1944 to fight through the backbone of our adversaries' winter line defenses, setting the scene for the new challenge before us—what would prove to be the four battles of Monte Cassino.

The magnitude of the task was apparent from the outset. The rugged terrain, coupled with the formidable German defenses, presented an almost insurmountable obstacle. Yet, I knew it was my responsibility to inspire my men and lead them forward despite the odds.

The initial assaults on Monte Cassino were intense. The cacophony of artillery barrages, small arms fire, and wounded soldiers' screams created a harrowing atmosphere. I had been tasked with coordinating our movements, ensuring my men stayed focused in the face of fierce resistance.

The most poignant moment in that months-long battle was the bombing of the Monte Cassino Abbey in February. It was a moment forever seared in my memory. The abbey, perched atop a historic hilltop and founded centuries ago by a Benedictine monk, stood as a symbol of peace. Yet, on that fateful day, it became a casualty of conflict.

"Sir, are you sure it's necessary to destroy the abbey?" I asked in a message to the colonel leading our battalion. "It's a protected historic zone."

"We are aware of that, captain," he replied. "But our leaders are convinced it's being utilized by the enemy as an observation post. So the abbey must be destroyed."

My men and I watched horrified as Allied bombs crumbled the majestic structure. Steeped in centuries of history and tradition, the abbey was reduced to rubble before our eyes. Needless to say, it took a toll on us emotionally and spiritually.

As we marched past the devastation, I couldn't help feeling sadness and regret over the loss of such a cherished landmark. In that moment, the true cost of war became painfully clear to us all.

Despite the destruction of the abbey, the German defenders remained entrenched in the rough terrain, blocking our Allied forces' advance to Rome. Our subsequent assaults proved to be incredibly costly. The relentless fighting—involving close-quarters combat and hand-to-hand skirmishes—tested the mettle of even the bravest soldiers. Every day I was forced to make difficult decisions, weighing the risks and rewards of each maneuver as we fought ferociously for every inch of ground.

Whenever we got a brief respite, I would gather my platoon and check in with them.

"Okay, boys, I just want to see how you're holding up. It's important during this long, bitter campaign that we remain strong for each other. And we must draw our courage from our trust in God, and from each other, finding hope in the face of adversity."

Ultimately, the Allied forces captured Monte Cassino in the fourth and final battle. It was a hard-won victory, achieved through sacrifice and perseverance. It was during the final days of that battle that our regiment learned we were being called up for "Operation Overlord."

As pre-dawn darkness enveloped the English Channel on June 6, 1944, I stood on the deck of our landing craft gazing at the distant shores of Normandy. I was leading my men as part of the initial Allied landing force for "Operation Overlord," codename for the Battle of Normandy.

Our anticipation was palpable as we approached the coast of France, listening to the rumble of the naval bombardment in the distance. We knew the risks ahead—the German defenses, the fortified bunkers, the mines littering the beaches— but we were unwavering in our mission to liberate Europe from tyranny.

As the landing craft lurched forward, the battle erupted around us. The air was thick with the rain of small arms fire, and the sky was illuminated by the repeated explosive flashes. Our landing craft hit the beach with a jolt, lowered the ramp, and exposed us to the full fury of enemy fire.

With adrenaline coursing through my veins, I led my men as we advanced under withering hostile fire. Yes, we had trained for this moment, but nothing could prepare us for what we now faced. The beach was a hellish nightmare of destruction, littered with the wreckage of landing craft and the bodies of casualties, too numerous to count.

We pushed through a maelstrom of gunfire and explosions. The air was thick with the acrid smell of gunpowder melded with the smell of death. It was a battle of inches as I shouted orders over the din, rallying my men to keep moving forward.

Suddenly, I felt a searing pain in my side. The world began to spin as I stumbled and fell to the ground. I realized I had been hit as I watched the blood stain on my uniform grow larger. But despite the pain, I knew I had to keep going—my men were counting on me. Unfortunately, my legs suddenly buckled under me.

Donny was by my side and helped me crawl to the safety of a nearby crater. But the battle raged on around us, and I knew we couldn't stay there long. My men needed leadership, and I needed to find a way to get back to them.

Operating on pure adrenaline, I pushed myself to my feet with Donny's help and staggered forward. Every step was agony, but I refused to give up. I could hear the shouts of my men in the distance, and I knew I had to reach them.

As I stumbled through the smoke and debris, I felt a hand on my shoulder. It was Rob. He had come back to find me.

"Captain, we've got you," he said, his voice steady despite the horrendous scene around us. "We're going to get you out of here."

Rob, Donny, and a few other brave souls from my platoon, hoisted me onto their shoulders and carried me back toward our lines. It felt like an eternity as we made our way through the battlefield. Bullets zipped past us, and explosions rocked the ground, but the men never faltered.

Medics were waiting to tend my wounds once we reached the aid station. As they patched me up and loaded me onto a stretcher, I looked up at the faces of the men who had risked their lives to save mine. They were exhausted, bloodied, but unbowed—true heroes in every sense of the word.

And then I blacked out.

I, along with many other injured soldiers, was loaded onto an LST and transported back to the coast of England. Eventually, my stretcher was transferred to a train bound for one of the 150-plus American-built hospitals scattered across the British countryside.

I was taken to the 186th General Hospital near the Fairford train station in the Cotswolds, about an hour outside of London. The surgical team removed the shrapnel that had wreaked havoc in my body, repaired the damage to my organs, and patched me up. My surgery lasted four hours.

I never really had an opportunity to thank the surgical team that saved my life, but I will forever be in their debt. I do, however, know the name of the one who greeted me when I first opened my eyes in the recovery ward. At first, I thought I must have died and gone to heaven because she looked like an angel.

Though I gained consciousness for only a moment, it was long enough to see her smile and hear her tender voice: "Captain Fearsithe, you're going to be okay. My name is Nurse Dodd, and I'm going to be taking care of you. Go back to sleep and get some rest."

∾

9

MONDAY, JUNE 12 – FRIDAY, DECEMBER 1, 1944

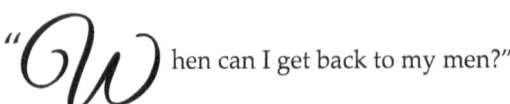

"When can I get back to my men?"

I was still drifting in and out of consciousness, but that was the most important question on my mind. I didn't ask about the extent of my injuries, and being discharged and going back home never crossed my mind. I needed to get back to my band of brothers. I was their leader, and I was not about to shirk my duty.

"That's between you and your doctor," Nurse Dodd replied, after I had asked her for the third time.

"What day is it anyway?" I asked now that I knew she could answer me.

"It's Sunday, June 18," she answered. "Your surgery took place a week ago. And from what I've been told, you are pretty lucky to still be alive, captain."

"June 18!?" I shouted. "That means I've been away from my men for almost two weeks! You need to get me out of here!"

"Captain, you're not even able to get out of bed right now," the nurse replied. "You underwent extensive surgery to repair your liver, spleen, and kidneys. Your body needs time to recover! What good do you think you would be to your men right now?"

I guess she had me there. As I stared up at her from my bed, I realized she was an attractive young woman—not the matronly disciplinarian I had pictured. She looked to be about my age, with blue eyes, and blonde curls protruding from the edges of her nurse's Flossie. She was what the boys in my platoon would call a "real dish." However, I knew despite her delicate appearance, she was more than capable of putting me in my place. I decided I admired that about her.

"Do you have any news on how our boys are doing down on Omaha Beach?" I asked, a little less demanding as I changed the subject.

"I overheard a couple of officers talking this morning," Nurse Dodd replied, "and they were saying the tide was turning in our favor. The beachhead has been secured, and our troops are pushing inland. They thought we had certainly taken the first crucial step toward victory."

"That's certainly good news!" I declared. "We have to keep the Germans on the run, all the way back to Berlin! Is there any way I can find out how my men are doing?"

"I can't help you with that information, captain. But I will make sure the briefing officer knows of your request."

"Thank you, nurse. You sound like you're a Southern gal. What's your name, and where are you from?"

"My name is Elizabeth, and I'm from Richmond, Virginia!" she replied with obvious pride. "Have you ever been there?"

"I passed by there on my way to basic training a couple of years ago," I told her. "But we didn't really go through Richmond. Actually, before joining the Army, I had never been south of Pennsylvania."

"Well, when the war is over, you'll have to come visit our fair city," Nurse Dodd remarked. "In fact, you should really visit in the spring. There isn't any place prettier than Richmond in the spring!"

"I'll make a point to do that one day!" I replied with a smile. "Perhaps you could give me a tour."

She smiled at my comment, then went about her duties. As my days of convalescing turned into weeks, Nurse Dodd and I enjoyed frequent conversations. When my strength returned, I took many leisurely strolls with her through the hospital's garden. Initially she walked with me to keep me steady on my feet, but it soon became more than that. The garden became "our" place—the one patch of ground untouched by the war.

The more Nurse Dodd and I talked, the deeper our conversations became —what our lives would be like in a world free of war's death and oppression. We even dared to talk about our respective future plans after the war.

The doctors were pleased with my recovery but insisted I needed to heal completely before they would release me for active duty. I had now been in the hospital more than four months—with no end in sight.

～

Lizzie, as I now called her, was on duty when a kerfuffle broke out about how to treat a new patient. She had just met with the head nurse to discuss a matter of protocol. Afterward, she stepped outside to clear her head and saw me sitting in what had become my chair in the garden.

"You will not believe what's happening," she said as she walked over. "An officer has just entered into the surgical theater with severe injuries. But, apparently, no one at the hospital seemed to know that the lieutenant was colored until he arrived. Though the surgical team doesn't seem to have an issue with it, the administrative staff is beside itself as to what to do with a colored patient. Though our staff has been vaguely aware of the Army's initiatives to integrate the races, it hasn't been anything we have been prepared to participate in."

"So what's the plan?" I asked.

"No one is sure," Lizzie replied. "The most pressing need is blood. The surgeons told the administrators to get it—and they weren't about to take no for an answer. The hospitals providing integrated care have established separate blood banks. We neither have the time nor the people to do that."

"Well, I can help," I replied. "I'll donate some blood."

"But you don't know if you're even a match!"

"You forget, nurse, I'm O negative—a universal donor," I replied with a grin. "Get me hooked up. I'm probably good for at least two pints!"

"That might not be enough."

"Well, aren't there others in this hospital who can give blood?" I asked. "I thought you all operated under a Hippocratic oath or something! Isn't anyone else a universal donor?"

"I am," she said weakly.

"Well, there you go! Now there are two of us, and we haven't even begun to ask around. Let's get moving, nurse!"

I got up from my chair and started to walk inside. Lizzie hesitated a moment before a smile settled on her face. "Yes, let's get going, captain!"

The head nurse didn't quite know what to think of us when Lizzie told her we were willing to donate blood. Nevertheless, after a few minutes of hesitation she had us set up. Soon I noticed a few other hospital workers volunteering to donate.

"We solved that problem," I said to Lizzie with a grin as we sat there with needles stuck in our arms. "What other problem needs to be tackled?"

"There is still the issue of a place in the ward for him to recover."

"You mean they're having trouble finding a bed?" I declared in disbelief. "It's a big ward! Surely no one has a problem with him stretching out on a bed in the ward. And if they're running short, he can have my bed!"

"It's not a bed we need," Lizzie said sadly, "it's a separate ward."

"Lizzie, that's wrong!" I said indignantly. "This guy was injured while fighting for his country—and for freedom—and now this hospital doesn't want to give him a bed because he has to be placed in a separate ward? That's crazy! What's more, it's immoral!"

Lizzie didn't know how to respond. We both stared at one another for a moment. Then an idea came to me.

"Then let's make a separate ward," I said with determination. "You move two beds—one for him and one for me—into a corner and put some curtains around them. And he and I will have our own private ward!"

Believe it or not, that is exactly what the hospital did! There were other obstacles that Lizzie and I helped them overcome, including who would provide nursing care for the lieutenant. Lizzie and I volunteered to be the attendants in our private ward. She would be the professional, and I would be her lackey.

The colored officer was in surgery for many hours, and his face and right side were heavily bandaged when they finally wheeled him into our makeshift ward. He was still out of it from the anesthesia.

"By the way, what's this soldier's name?" I asked Lizzie.

She looked down at his paperwork and replied, "Lt. Larnell Williams."

I could not believe my ears or eyes. I just stood there looking at Larnell lying in that bed, and for the first time since hearing of his arrival, I did something I should have done much earlier: I lifted up a prayer for my injured comrade. And I asked God to forgive us for being unwilling to help this poor man—my friend—when he needed us most!

I later learned that on October 5, a battalion from the Ninety-Second Infantry Division entered into actual combat for the first time in the war.

They joined the attack on the Axis forces along the coast of the Ligurian Sea near the town of Massa. Despite the battalion being under-supported, the Alpha Platoon, under the command of First Lieutenant Larnell Williams, rallied the others in making great gains during the initial stages of battle.

Seven days later, still without artillery or air support, those gains were turned back by enemy counterattacks. All the men of Alpha Platoon were either severely wounded or killed. Lieutenant Williams was transported to the 186th General Hospital for treatment due to the severity of his dental and facial injuries.

Major Schwartz and Captain Felt, Larnell's primary surgeons, came by our makeshift ward to check on their patient a couple hours following surgery. I introduced myself and told them Larnell and I were friends from the same hometown and had gone through OCS together. "How is he, docs?" I asked. "Is he going to make it?"

Major Schwartz answered, "Captain Fearsithe, do you believe in God?"

"I most definitely do," I responded. "I know for certain I wouldn't be standing here today if it weren't for Him."

"Well, Captain Fearsithe," the major replied, "I don't think your friend would still be with us if God had not placed you in this hospital. We heard what you and Nurse Dodd did. If you had not volunteered your blood when you did, Lieutenant Williams would not have survived surgery. So, I will tell you that he has a better chance of making it now than I would have given him a few hours ago.

"But I won't lie to you, his injuries were severe. The reconstruction that Captain Felt did on his face and jaw was extensive. He has a long, steep road ahead, and many more surgeries in his future."

The Major instructed Lizzie what she should be watching for as the lieutenant's anesthesia wore off. The doctor encouraged her to be generous with the morphine to manage his pain during the first few days.

It quickly became obvious that Larnell was going to require more care than I could provide, both from a physical and knowledge standpoint. Gratefully, one of the other nurses agreed to assist Lizzie.

Several days into his recovery, Larnell made a subtle movement that indicated he could hear me speaking to Lizzie. I wondered if he had recognized my voice, so I walked over to the side of his bed.

Leaning down close to his face, I said, "Larnell, it's me, Bobby. I am right here with you, man! And I've got your back. I'm in the bed right next to you, and I'm not going anywhere. And you need to know your nurses are the best in this place. You're going to get better, my friend!"

I saw a teardrop in the small space under his left eye that wasn't covered with bandages—and I knew he had heard me. I grasped his left hand and felt a weak squeeze in return. A tear trickled down my cheek as I offered up a silent prayer.

Larnell's discomfort diminished as the days passed. He became more aware of his extensive injuries—including the inability to move his jaw to speak, which made communication challenging. With much effort, he eventually was able to use his left hand to write out short messages on a clipboard. This made day-to-day functions somewhat easier for him and the nurses.

I sat by his bed and talked to him every day. I shared any gossip I heard from the hospital staff. I recounted news about the war. I talked about our times together at Fort Benning. And on the days we received mail, I read the news from home—written by my mother or his. He asked that I start writing letters from him to his mother. He would write out a few words on his clipboard, and I would fill in the details.

Though I thought I knew Larnell pretty well from our time at OCS, I really got to know him through his letters from his mother. She wrote about memories of good times at home and about his dreams for the future. She caught him up on all the news about his younger sister, as well as their extended family.

She described different happenings in Williamsport. But the more I read, the more I realized the city Larnell grew up in was totally different from my experience. And while some of that was to be expected, much of it was just wrong. He and I had worked together in a lumberyard, but I hadn't really known him. It was as if we lived in two different places and I had never cared enough to ask why or to really get to know him. And I think in some respects, Larnell might have said the same thing ... but maybe not.

All I knew was, I was getting to know this mother's oldest child through her eyes—a young man she was extremely proud of and whom she loved more than life.

By the end of November, I received splendid news.

"Well, Captain Fearsithe, looks like you'll be leaving us in a few days," my doctor told me. "You can return to active duty once we discharge you."

"That's great news, doc! I can't wait to be back with my men!"

However, my zeal was tempered by my thoughts of saying goodbye to Lizzie and Larnell. I was more determined than ever to see this war ended soon so I could make my way back to Lizzie, either here or in Richmond.

Our relationship had blossomed during our many long walks and numerous conversations. She was now one of the main people in my life for whom I would be fighting. And I would be the soldier she constantly worried about.

I wanted to ask Lizzie to marry me before I left the hospital; however, I hesitated to ask knowing I was going back to the front line. I didn't want her to feel obligated in case something happened to me. So, whether it was right or wrong, I stopped short of saying those words the day I left.

I had no doubts that God had brought me to the 186th General Hospital so I would meet and fall in love with Lizzie. Now I was going to have to trust Him to bring us back together.

Similarly, the same was true with Larnell. I wouldn't be here to help him during his recovery. But Lizzie and others would, so I knew he would be in good hands. In the last letter I read to Larnell from his mother, she said she would be praying for me. I knew I could use all the prayers I could get!

On Friday, December 1, I was discharged and tried not to look back. I was headed to Belgium to join back up with my men.

10

SATURDAY, DECEMBER 2, 1944 – TUESDAY, JULY 31, 1945

~

I arrived in Eupen, Belgium, the morning of December 2 and reported to Lt. Colonel Learnard. This region was where exhausted troops came to enjoy some respite so they could leave the war behind for a short while and recharge.

While I was in the hospital convalescing, the First Division had incurred significant losses in the Battle of Hürtgen Forest, located just east of the Belgian-German border. U.S. commanders recognized the division's need to rest after such a hard-fought battle and ordered them to Eupen. A change of the divisional command had also just occurred, transitioning from General Clarence Huebner to General Clift Andrus.

"Welcome back, captain," Colonel Learnard said as I walked into his hut. "Did they put you back together with all the right parts?"

"As best I can tell, sir," I answered with a grin. "Hopefully the ones they had left over weren't important."

"As long as they didn't leave out that sharp mind of yours, we'll allow for some margin of error," he replied, returning the grin. "Are you ready to get back in command?"

"Yes, sir!" I answered briskly. "I think the doctors and nurses at Fairfield were tired of me hounding them about when I could return!"

"Well, good!" the colonel said. "That's the spirit! We can definitely use you. Your platoon has performed well under Rob Smith. As a matter of fact, I promoted him to captain soon after we shipped you off. And, by the way, here's a golden oak leaf to replace those bars you're wearing. I recommended a promotion for you as well. It was approved back in September, and I've been holding your oak leaf for you. Congratulations, Major Fearsithe!"

"I don't know what to say, sir," I replied.

"Don't say anything. You earned it. After all this division has accomplished under officers like you, I don't think the Pentagon can issue promotions fast enough! Well done, major!"

"Thank you, sir!" I said. "Whatever I have accomplished is because of a great commander like you and an incomparable team like my platoon!"

"And modest as well," Col. Leonard said with a smile. "I agree, there are a number of fine men in Alpha Platoon. But I also know that their excellent performance reflects your leadership.

"Now then, let's talk about your next assignment. I'm putting you in command of First Rifle Company—which, as you know, includes your old platoon. I'm transferring its current company commander, Major Stan Jones, to the Fourth Heavy Weapons Company. The assignment will better fit his skills, plus the First needs a leader who is agile and decisive. I have no doubt you will lead it well. Report to the First Company's command hut and assume leadership. Any questions?"

"Only one, sir," I asked. "When do we get our next orders?"

"Any day now, major! Make sure your soldiers are ready. This break will soon be over."

While we waited for our orders, I got acquainted with all my platoon captains as well as reconnected with Rob and the rest of Alpha Platoon. Each man in the unit had aged in the six months since I last saw him. They had fought ferociously to gain ground in France from Omaha Beach to Belgium—and they had witnessed atrocities no man should see. Each one had suffered some type of battle wound—some unseeable by the naked eye.

All of them had stories to tell about their experiences—which they would never be able to share with someone who wasn't there.

As I looked at Donny, in particular, I remembered the promise his mother had asked of me three long years earlier: "Bring him home to me, Bobby." The man standing in front of me wasn't the indecisive, naïve, young man she had been referring to that evening. He had changed—some for the good, and perhaps some for the not so good—but there was no going back. Then again, that was probably true for all of us. Would any of our mothers even recognize us?

Over the next few days an unseasonably harsh winter pushed into the region, bringing heavy snow, ice, and temperatures below zero. Weather forecasters were describing it as Europe's coldest and harshest winter in history. Our Air Force remained on the ground due to low visibility.

The German army launched a surprise offensive on December 16 into eastern Belgium and northeastern France, creating a bulge in our Allied front lines. (A bulge is part of a defensive line that juts into enemy territory like a peninsula into the sea, leaving that section vulnerable on three sides). At 0530 we awoke to a massive ninety-minute artillery barrage. Our division was immediately called up to hold the "northern shoulder of the bulge" in Büllingen/Bütgenbach, Belgium, about twenty miles from Eupen.

We arrived the next day, just in time to force the German Panzer Division leading the assault to turn aside from the primary road through Bütgenbach onto the poor, secondary roads to the south and west. This move slowed their progress and enabled our other divisions to establish defensive positions along the perimeter.

During the week of Christmas, our regiment—assisted by artillery and tank destroyer units—again successfully fought off determined German tank and infantry assaults aimed at opening up the main road. The intense fighting continued for several weeks despite the deepening snow and bitter cold.

By January 15, the German advance had lost its momentum, and their soldiers began to retreat to Germany. Our forces began a counteroffensive in pursuit. On January 29, we retook Büllingen, then four days later crossed into Germany penetrating their formidable Siegfried line of defenses along the border. We knew the end of the war was in sight!

First Rifle Company, together with the rest of our regiment, arrived at the town of Remagen in mid-March. The Germans had failed to demolish the Ludendorff Bridge prior to its capture by our Ninth Armored Division. Our orders were to secure the bridge so six of our divisions (totaling 125,000 men), together with tanks, artillery pieces, and trucks, could safely travel across.

The atmosphere was tense as we took up our positions on the eastern bank of the Rhine River, facing down the might of the German army. Colonel Learnard told us if our mission was successful, it would accelerate the Allied advance into Germany and shorten the war.

The Germans knew that as well! They were relentless in their attempts to destroy the bridge, launching wave after wave of attacks using virtually every weapon at their disposal. To protect the bridge against aircraft, we positioned a large concentration of anti-aircraft weapons—leading to what was later called "the greatest anti-aircraft battle in history." The ground shook as explosions rocked the area around us. The air was thick with smoke and dust, which hampered our visibility.

Despite the bedlam and danger, our men stood firm, determined to hold the line at all costs. We returned fire with everything we had, raining down ordnance on the enemy forces in a desperate bid to keep them at bay. All around me I heard the voices of my men encouraging one another.

"Incoming mortar fire! Take cover!"

"We can't let up now! Keep firing, men! Every round counts!"

"They're throwing everything they've got at us, but we're holding strong!"

"I'm running low on ammo. Anyone got any spare clips?"

"Here, take these. We need every gun blazing if we're going to hold them off!"

"Keep your heads down! We've got wounded here that need tending."

"Medics! We need support over here!"

"We can't let them breach our lines! If they get through, it's all over!"

"Hold the line, men! Our brothers are counting on us to keep this bridge secure!"

"We've faced worse than this before! We can't falter now!"

"Keep up the pressure! Show those Krauts what we're made of!"

"That's it, boys! Keep pouring it on! Remember why we're here! We fight for freedom and for each other!"

"We're not giving an inch! Not today, not ever!"

As the hours stretched into days, the strain began to take its toll. Ammunition ran low, and many of our men were wounded or killed in the relentless barrage of enemy fire. But still we held on, refusing to give an inch to the enemy.

In the end, our efforts were not in vain. The Ludendorff Bridge stood firm for two days, providing sufficient time for those six divisions to pass over it. On the third day, it collapsed due to structural fatigue caused by the damage it had already experienced through the prior demolition efforts. Sadly, 200 brave Army engineers and welders, who were still working on the bridge when it collapsed, fell to their deaths.

The feat was a testament to the courage and determination of all those who had defended it against overwhelming odds. And though the cost was high, we knew our sacrifice helped pave the way for victory over Nazi Germany.

By spring, we marched with a renewed fervor for freedom and democracy, advancing into the heart of Germany with our boots pounding against the war-torn landscapes of Europe. With each step forward, we left behind a trail of liberated towns and villages, pushing back the darkness of tyranny and oppression.

We continued to engage in fierce combat skirmishes against a determined German resistance. Across the open fields of the Rhineland, we faced enemy fire with steely determination, our rifles blazing as they cleared out enemy strongholds and secured vital objectives.

After we received word that Adolf Hitler had committed suicide, and as the world held its breath, we witnessed the collapse of the Nazi regime. But we also bore witness to the horrors of the Holocaust as we liberated and provided aid to concentration camp survivors. Every soldier to a man was devastated as he realized the atrocities these people had been forced to suffer.

"I can't believe a human being is capable of doing that to another human being," I said quietly to Rob as I surveyed the hundreds of walking skeletons.

He just stood there with tears in his eyes, too overcome to speak.

When Germany finally surrendered on May 8, my company was ordered to carry out occupation duties. We were transported to Wiesbaden to maintain order and ensure residents complied with the surrender terms. The city, once a bustling hub of activity, now displayed the scars of war—streets lined with rubble and buildings bearing the wounds of conflict.

I spent my days overseeing the transition from wartime chaos to post-war stability. My fellow officers and I worked tirelessly to restore order and rebuild the shattered infrastructure of the cities. Our mission was clear: to help Germany recover and pave the way for a peaceful and prosperous future.

One of my primary responsibilities was liaising with local authorities and community leaders to coordinate reconstruction efforts. Together, we worked to clear debris, repair damaged buildings, and restore essential services such as water, electricity, and transportation.

It was a daunting task, but one that filled me with a sense of purpose knowing our efforts were helping to rebuild lives and communities. On more than one occasion, I drew from the construction experience I had gleaned at Lundy Lumber—though those memories felt like a lifetime ago.

I also was tasked with maintaining security and stability in the occupied territory. I worked closely with our Allied forces and the local German police to ensure law and order, and prevent a resurgence of Nazi sympathizers.

But perhaps the most rewarding part of my job was interacting with the locals. Despite the hardships they had endured, the people of Wiesbaden greeted us with warmth and hospitality. We worked side by side, forging bonds of friendship and mutual respect as we rebuilt their city together.

As the dust settled in the wake of Nazi defeat, the transition in local city government unfolded like a symphony of hope amid the ruins of a shattered past. The first step was the dissolution of Nazi leadership, a resounding declaration that the era of tyranny had come to an end. Like dominoes falling, individuals tainted by Nazi affiliation were removed, their grip on power loosened by the winds of change.

But the true crescendo of this symphony came with the process of de-Nazi-fication, a profound reckoning with the sins of the past. It was a journey into the heart of darkness as investigators combed through the tangled web of Nazi influence, seeking to untangle the threads of complicity. Those responsible for war crimes and atrocities were brought to justice, their offenses laid bare for all to see.

Following the removal of Nazi officials, a new Germany began to emerge —one of renewal and rejuvenation. New leaders stepped forward to take the reins of local government. They were the harbingers of change, guiding their communities towards a brighter future free from the shackles of the past.

One of those new leaders was Herr Heinrich Schmidt, a schoolteacher in his late fifties and a most affable fellow. Somehow, he and his wife had dodged the stain of Nazi ideology. They saw the day the armistice was signed as a day of emancipation from oppression.

The Schmidts were determined to do whatever they could to help their city return to kinder and gentler days. They were instrumental in locating a pastor who had been a leader of the Confessing Church, an anti-Nazi evangelical congregation. They successfully invited him to come to Wies-baden to reopen the doors of the First Lutheran Church.

"Why did you search outside of your city for a pastor?" I asked Heinrich.

"Because the Nazis drove all the Bible-believing, Bible-preaching pastors out of our pulpits," he answered. "The men left were merely puppets for Nazi propaganda."

Once the church reopened, Heinrich joined the new city council and set about doing his part to rebuild the city. Displaced persons began to find refuge in the embrace of the community, and the economy slowly began to stir from its slumber.

As the days turned into weeks and months, steady signs of progress emerged across the region. Streets were bustling as shops reopened, and life slowly returned to normal. Schools were rebuilt, and children played in the parks once again, their laughter a testament to the resilience of the human spirit.

Nevertheless, there were reminders of the war's toll—empty stares of those who had lost loved ones, haunted expressions of survivors who bore physical and emotional scars of conflict. It was a sobering reminder of the price of war.

As I walked the streets of Wiesbaden, I couldn't help but feel hopeful for the future. I prayed that we had learned valuable lessons from this war: to resolve our differences peacefully and to prevent tyrants from gaining positions of control. Despite the challenges that lay ahead, I knew if we stood united, we could overcome any obstacle and build a better world for generations to come.

∿

11

WEDNESDAY, AUGUST 1 – FRIDAY, DECEMBER 21, 1945

~

he frantic pace of our lives, plus the challenges of mail delivery to and from a war zone, meant Lizzie and I had been able to exchange only an occasional letter. However, once I arrived in Wiesbaden, our correspondence became more regular. My work schedule became more settled, and Lizzie's patient load lessened.

I received the following on August 1:

July 24, 1945

Dear Bobby,

The 186th General Hospital officially closed its doors to new patients last night at 2400 hours. Major Schwartz met with the nurses yesterday and told us he expected the last patient would either be released or transferred out by August 10. He thinks those of us who are here until the end will be transported back to the U.S. on August 12. It's hard to imagine!

Larnell sends his greetings. He is recovering well from his fourth reconstructive surgery. He'll still need to have cosmetic surgery when he gets back to the States, but at least everything is now beginning to heal. He is able to eat soft foods, and his speech is more understandable. He is still fighting depression, but overall his outlook is improving.

He confided that he has mixed feelings about getting back home and seeing his family. I told him you said you were praying for him. I think he will be transported to the States on August 4 with the rest of our severely injured patients.

Daddy wrote and said he and my mother are planning a special party to welcome me home. They plan to invite anyone who is anyone in Richmond to attend. I told him I didn't want any big to-do, but you know how that was received! It went in one ear and out the other!

I sure wish we could see each other before I go back to the U.S., but I know your orders will not permit. I'm still hoping you are back stateside by Christmas so we can be together over the holidays.

I miss you. If I were a praying person, I would tell you I'm praying for you—like you always tell me. But know that you are always in my thoughts.

L,

Lizzie

She always signed off her letters to me with "L." Lizzie explained that since we hadn't actually said we love each other yet, and she knew she liked me, "L" would have to do for now!

Her comment about seeing each other before she returned stateside made me wonder if I could get a few days' leave. I wouldn't be able to see Larnell before he was transferred out, but maybe I could see Lizzie before she left. The transition in Wiesbaden was going smoothly, and a brief absence would be a good test to see how things functioned without me. Colonel Learnard had recently transferred to the nearby city of Frankfurt, overseeing the transition there, so I sent him a request.

I received his favorable response the next day, so I quickly set out looking for air transportation to Fairfield. I was excited to find a plane from Frankfurt airfield to London, departing the morning of August 5.

When the jeep arrived to take me to Frankfurt, Heinrich and his wife were there to see me off. She presented me with one of her freshly baked chocolate cakes, carefully wrapped in cloth to protect it for the journey.

"You can't go visit your fräulein without a gift for her," she said with a smile. I realized the Schmidts were starting to think of themselves as my surrogate parents—and Frau Schmidt was helping me avoid making a social faux pas.

As I returned her heartfelt hug and accepted her kind gift with thanks, I realized the three of us were a picture of emerging Deutsch-English relations. Unfortunately for me, Frau Schmidt's mouthwatering baked goods were quickly adding pounds to my waistline!

Upon my arrival in London, I was able to catch a train to Fairfield Station, arriving at the hospital early that afternoon to Lizzie's great surprise. The hospital was functioning at a much slower pace now, so Lizzie's supervisor gave her the afternoon off.

Nestled amid rolling hills and meandering streams, the town of Fairfield had mostly remained unscathed by the war. The afternoon sun cast its golden glow on the cobblestone streets as Lizzie and I strolled hand in hand to the town square. I admired the town's Victorian charm, complete with quaint cottages adorned by blooming roses.

We paused by the ancient stone bridge that spanned the tranquil brook, its waters shimmering like liquid silver in the sunlight. Leaning against the weathered parapet, we shared stories from our time apart as we sampled Frau Schmidt's delicious chocolate cake. Neither Lizzie nor I talked about the harsh realities we had experienced as a result of the war. For now, we wanted to share only good things—those rare, beautiful moments that bloomed even in the adversity of war.

Our walk continued through fields of swaying wheat and meadows ablaze with wildflowers, the scent of summer mingling with the warmth of our affection. As each minute passed, we felt the weight of separation lift from our shoulders, replaced by a sense of joy.

As the afternoon waned and the sky turned shades of orange and pink, we found ourselves atop a hill overlooking the town. We watched as the sun dipped below the horizon, casting a fiery glow across the landscape.

In that moment, surrounded by the beauty of Fairfield, I knew it was the right time to tell Lizzie how I felt. Love—even unspoken—was a force stronger than any war, a beacon that had guided us to each other. We walked back toward the heart of town, our hearts intertwined, confessing our love for one another and knowing that it would endure.

Our immediate plans, however, were still in the hands of the Army. Lizzie, together with most of the other remaining medical staff, was being transferred to McGuire General Hospital in her hometown of Richmond, Virginia. Many of the remaining patients in Fairfield had already been, or soon would be, going to that facility, including Larnell.

I was headed back to Wiesbaden the next day—for how long, I didn't know. I'd heard a rumor that some of us may make it home by Christmas, while others would be needed into next year. Several of us had also heard the war in the Pacific would soon be over. It was being widely reported that one of our bombers had dropped an atomic bomb on Hiroshima, Japan, the day after I had arrived in Fairfield.

Descriptions we heard of the devastation it caused were beyond comprehension. I thanked God that no such bomb was dropped here in Europe, though it was widely reported that Adolf Hitler had his scientists feverishly working on one.

The world was a far different place from what it had been before this war began—World War II they now called it. Unlike what happened after the First World War, a post-war economic boom was already in sight. Lizzie excitedly talked about my coming to Richmond to meet her parents once I got stateside.

"There will be all kinds of opportunities in Richmond for a decorated war hero like you," she gushed. "And my daddy will be able to introduce you into all the right circles."

"It seems someone has already started making plans for our future," I replied with a grin. "Let's not get ahead of ourselves."

"Okay, but a girl can dream, can't she?" Lizzie asked as she batted those pretty blues at me.

The next morning we kissed goodbye and I returned to Wiesbaden. I was encouraged to discover there had been no problems during my absence. Rob and Heinrich teased that I had simply become an unnecessary layer of management. However, the next morning proved that our celebration was somewhat premature.

A group of German civilians was tired of waiting for permission to salvage belongings from their homes, which were now reduced to rubble. This particular area had been deemed unsafe, so no one could enter without permission. Among the salvagers was Liesl Müller, a widowed mother of two, determined to retrieve her family's precious heirlooms buried beneath the rubble.

At the heart of the conflict lay the struggle for survival and dignity. Our soldiers had been instructed to keep the area free of intruders; the Germans failed to see themselves as intruders. An already tense situation boiled over on this scorching hot summer day as troops tried to balance security with meeting human needs.

As Liesl and her neighbors approached the property, they were confronted by soldiers enforcing strict regulations on looting. Misunderstandings quickly escalated into a heated exchange, fueled by language barriers and cultural differences.

The soldiers, ever vigilant for any potential resurgence of Nazi sentiment, viewed the civilians' actions with suspicion and questioned their motives. Liesl and her compatriots viewed the soldiers as trespassers, interfering with residents' efforts to reclaim precious possessions after patiently waiting for weeks.

I received a message over the radio as the situation escalated. In the background, I heard shouts of frustration mingled with the cries of children caught in the verbal crossfire of conflicting agendas.

I arrived at the scene with Heinrich in tow as the standoff was reaching its climax. I appealed to both sides to calm down so we could come up with a rational solution. Heinrich learned that Liesl's oldest son was turning six years old the following day.

"The boy told his mother he wants his futbol," Heinrich relayed.

"That is no problem," I said. "We can find him a futbol."

"No, you don't understand," Heinrich replied, "he wants his futbol. His father gave it to him before he left for war. The boy only wants that futbol."

The boy's request, the mother's frantic effort, and the crowd's earnestness had now been made clear to all of us. I immediately arranged for an engineering team to come make the needed structural arrangements so the damaged home was safe to enter. Afterward, I gave Liesl and a few of her friends permission to enter. Within a matter of minutes, a shout went up— the ball had been found!

It was a significant investment of resources for the sake of one used futball. But the goodwill it yielded was priceless. Frowns turned to smiles and shaking fists transformed into friendly waves, poignant reminders of the complexities inherent in post-war reconstruction. Liesl, her fellow citizens, and the soldiers on duty all learned a valuable lesson in communication and the trust, cooperation, and understanding that results from it.

On December 1, I received a pleasant surprise. Orders came through that I and the men who had come with me from Camp Blanding in 1942 were being transported on December 5 for final out-processing at Camp Kilmer in New Jersey. Of course, this did not include men who were choosing to reenlist. Though we had been told to expect a pre-Christmas discharge, I hadn't honestly believed it would happen.

I said goodbye to Heinrich and his wife, vowing to stay in touch.

"God truly blessed me with a set of parents on both continents. I promise I will return for 'family' visits," I told them, holding back tears.

Frau Schmidt wrapped her arms around me and drew me in so tightly, I thought she was never going to let me go.

Our two-week ocean voyage was slow and uneventful. Rob, Donny, and the rest of us played cards, slept, told jokes, and reflected on the memories of war that churned inside us. We were excited to be headed home together, but we were also a little apprehensive.

We shared things we had not shared with anyone else—and never would. We could tell others our stories, but only we would ever know their deeper meaning.

A wintry chill blanketed Camp Kilmer amid the bustling activity that morning. Now that we were here at the demobilization center to receive our final orders, we did so with a mixture of eagerness and uncertainty.

"Can you believe it?" I asked the men. "This moment has finally arrived."

"So, what's the first thing you guys are going to do when you get home?" Rob asked.

Donny, wearing a broad grin, was the first to answer.

"Sleep in a real bed, for starters. And maybe indulge in a home-cooked meal that doesn't come from a mess hall. But Bobby, that means I'll have to come over to your house since everyone knows my mom can't cook."

"Amen to that!" Jack added with a laugh. "But you know what I'm looking forward to the most? Just sitting on the porch with my girl, watching the sunset without a care in the world."

"Which girl is that?" Rob asked with a raised eyebrow.

"I haven't decided yet," Jack answered. "But I know she's very pretty."

"I'm sure she'll be pretty, Jack," I interjected. "What about you, Rob? What's first on your list?"

"Oh, you know me," he replied. "I'll probably fire up my old jalopy, take it out for a spin, and catch up with old friends. I might even see if the girl who turns down Jack wants to go for a spin with me!"

After the laughter died down, Rob asked, "What about you, Bobby? Are you headed down to Richmond for a visit?"

"I plan to spend Christmas with my folks in Williamsport," I said, "then drive down to Richmond for New Year's."

As I walked around Camp Kilmer, I thought of the men who had gone to war with us ... but had not returned. Men like Doug, Rick, and Bill. Each had willingly laid down his life and forfeited his opportunity to come back and kiss the girls, drive the cars, and live life to the fullest. I, for one, would never forget the sacrifice of those men.

But there was also a sense of relief. The war was over, and though the scars of conflict would linger, I was ready to embrace the promise of peace. As I received my discharge papers and stepped out into the crisp December air, I felt 100 pounds lighter. I exchanged handshakes and warm embraces with the men who had become such an integral part of my life for the past four years. I wondered if I would ever see most of them again.

The rest of the Williamsport crew and I made our way to our bus. Though the road to Williamsport would take us about five hours, it was just the beginning of a much longer journey. Our time in uniform had come to an end, but the lessons we learned would continue with us, a testament to God's grace and the bonds we had forged.

12

SATURDAY, DECEMBER 22 – MONDAY AFTERNOON, DECEMBER 24, 1945

❧

*T*he sun had already set when our bus rolled into Williamsport. Someone had obviously spread the word we were arriving that night. A "WELCOME HOME, HEROES" banner was held aloft by a large group of well-wishers, together with a contingent of the high school band dressed in uniform.

As soon as the driver turned off the engine, the band struck up an enthusiastic rendition of "God Bless America." Shouts and clapping from friends and family erupted as each of us stepped off the bus.

My mother reached me first and wrapped her arms around me. I lifted her off her feet and she gave me a squeeze that surpassed Frau Schmidt's. She wept as she whispered in my ear, "Welcome home, son! Thank You, God, for bringing him back to us!"

She finally released me long enough for my father to greet me. Though he was less emotional, he was by no means less sincere. "Welcome home, major!" he declared before crisply saluting me.

His salutation caught the attention of several other returning men, as well as some of the veteran fathers in the crowd. They all soon joined in the salute. The expression caught me by surprise, and I returned their salutes with a lump in my throat.

Just then a colored man and woman walked up to me.

"Major Fearsithe, you don't know us, but we know you," the man said. "I'm Clovis Williams and this here is my wife, Cora. Larnell is our son. We don't mean to take you away from your folks, but we wanted to thank you for what you have done for our son."

Mrs. Williams turned and looked at my mother. "Your son saved my Larnell's life."

I wanted to protest that I hadn't done anything special, but my heart compelled me to do something else instead. I reached out and placed my arms around Mrs. Williams and drew her in for a hug.

"Mrs. Williams," I said, "your son is one of the bravest and most dedicated men I have met in the Army. I am a better soldier and a better man because of him. I count it an honor to call him my friend, and if I was able to do anything for him, I can assure you it pales in the shadow of all he has taught me."

Then I backed away and saluted both of Larnell's parents, saying, "Please receive this salute on behalf of your son—Captain Williams."

I then introduced them to my mother and father, who acted pleased to meet the parents of the man I had told them so much about in my letters. Larnell's parents gave me a brief update on his medical condition before excusing themselves. I assured them I would drop by and see them soon.

Even though the night air was chilly, everyone seemed quite content to mingle there in the bus parking lot. It was a uniting moment. We had all shared a wartime experience—the soldiers in battle and the families in service at home. No one had escaped war's grip, but now we could finally celebrate its release.

One by one, families extended their best wishes and made their way to their vehicles. My parents and I were some of the last to leave. Since I was the senior ranking officer at the gathering, I felt a responsibility to thank each family.

The Buseys were already back home celebrating Donny's return by the time we got home. But as soon as we closed the front door, I heard a quiet knock. I opened it to find Mrs. Busey standing there.

"Bobby, you kept your promise," she said squeezing my hand. "You brought Donny home to me. Thank you!"

"Mrs. Busey," I replied, as I put my hand on top of hers, "truth be told, he brought me home. I wouldn't have made it without him. So, thank you, Mrs. Busey! Thank you, for letting him go."

A teardrop trickled down her cheek as she nodded and smiled. She gave my hand a final squeeze, then turned and walked back to her house to spend more time with her son.

I suddenly realized I was hungry as a pleasant aroma alerted me that my mother had obviously been cooking all day. She had prepared my favorite foods, and the three of us soon sat down to enjoy a delicious late supper. For a moment, I thought about the comment Donny had made about his mother's cooking. I smiled and wondered what the Buseys might be eating!

The next morning, I bound out of bed at my usual military time. I quickly realized the rest of the house was still asleep, so I quietly made my way downstairs, put on a pot of coffee, and decided to go for a run. It was still dark, but I could see the faint outline of unlit Christmas trees through the windows of many of the homes I passed and wreaths hanging from the window frames.

Some of the homes didn't have any up yet. But I knew that in most of those homes, the parents would stay up all night on Christmas Eve as Santa's helpers—putting up their decorations. The children in those homes would awaken to a Christmas splendor that would magically have appeared overnight. Though presents would still probably be sparse under the trees in all the homes this year, I was certain that each family would be enjoying a more plentiful and joyful Christmas than they had during the past few years.

By the time I got back home, the coffee was done, and my mother was in the kitchen preparing breakfast. I was glad for some time with just her; I wanted to talk to her about Lizzie.

"Do you have a picture of this southern Florence Nightingale?" Mom asked with a twinkle in her eye.

After I showed her my photograph of Lizzie, she said, "She is a very pretty young woman, and she sounds wonderful. When do you plan to see her again?"

"I want to get a car this week and drive to Richmond to see her on Saturday. I plan to stay for New Year's depending on what her family has planned. Would that be all right with you?"

"You're a grown man who has led hundreds of men into battle, so you don't need my permission. But I do have one question for you."

"What is it, Mom?"

"Lizzie sounds like a remarkable young woman, and from what you've told me she comes from a good family. She nursed you back to health and put her own life at risk to help others. She sounds like the best helpmate you could possibly find—except for one thing. What is her relationship with Jesus, Bobby? Of all the things you wrote about her, you never once mentioned her relationship with Him."

"We have talked about God, but she says her relationship with Him is a private one."

"I understand that some people prefer to demonstrate their love for God through their actions more than their words. But if the two of you are considering marriage, don't you think you need to know for certain that Jesus is the first relationship in both of your lives?"

When I hesitated to answer, she added, "Like I said, Bobby, you're a grown man. But if I were you, I'd want to know for certain."

"That's wise advice," I admitted. "I will discuss it with her next week."

After breakfast, the three of us went to Memorial Baptist Church. At my mom's request, I wore my dress uniform. The sanctuary was beautifully decorated for Christmas, just the way I had remembered it. Everyone extended a warm greeting to me, even those I didn't know. I was pleased to see Rob there with his family—also wearing his dress blues. He and I spoke briefly and arranged to meet at the Village Tea Room the next day for lunch.

Pastor Peterson made a point of welcoming us both back to church prior to the service. Next, he led the congregation in expressing their appreciation for our sacrifice by giving us a standing ovation.

After the congregational hymns and carols, the church choir erupted in a full-throated rendition of "O Holy Night," with the pastor's wife singing the solo. I couldn't help but note a glimmer of pride in Pastor Peterson's eyes.

The pastor's Christmas sermon stirred our hearts with the Good News of the Baby in the manger. He then challenged us to go out, like the shepherds of old, and convey the message of the Savior's birth to everyone we encountered. I noticed my mother looking at me out of the corner of her eye as the pastor made his remark.

Once again, my mom outdid herself by preparing my favorite dishes for Sunday dinner: roast beef, mashed potatoes and gravy, baby lima beans, and a lettuce wedge with blue cheese dressing. It was topped off with her homemade chocolate pie. I had not eaten a meal that delicious in four years, and I made sure my mom knew it!

Dad and I spent the remainder of the afternoon and evening talking about the war. I told him particular details surrounding the amphibious landings at Oran and Omaha Beach, as well as our protection of the Ludendorff Bridge. These were all military operations I knew would interest my engineering father. He listened to my accounts with clear attention to detail, asking for clarification as needed.

My mom walked into the room just as I was explaining about my injuries and the care I received.

"As I explained in my letters, I owe my life to Donny and Rob, as well as the rest of the men in my unit. They pulled me to safety and got me into the hands of the medics. I wouldn't have made it off the beach if it weren't for them."

I went on to describe my journey to the hospital at Fairfield as well as my surgery—at least the portions I could remember.

"There will always be lapses in my memory of those days," I clarified.

But the information that seemed to interest them most was my time with Larnell—both at Fort Benning and Fairfield Hospital. They were puzzled that we had been placed together in both situations.

"I've never heard of a white man and a colored man being thrust together like that," my mom remarked.

"What do you mean, 'thrust together,' Mom?"

"Well, I mean being forced to be roommates and spend all that time together and the like," she replied. "And I can't imagine being forced to give him your blood and care for him in the hospital."

"First of all, I wasn't forced to do anything; I was a willing participant. And quite frankly, I was honored to have been chosen at Fort Benning, and I felt blessed to be at Fairfield when Larnell was brought in. I saw God's hand in both instances. I wasn't there by chance. God had orchestrated for the two of us to be in those situations together.

"Larnell is now one of my best friends—as good a friend as Rob or Donny. Any one of the three would be willing to lay down his life for me—and me for any of them. Isn't that what Jesus teaches—that *greater love has no one than this, that someone lay down his life for his friends*?[1]

"And all I had to give was a few pints of blood!"

"I admire that, Bobby," my mom responded, "I really do. But I'm just saying that I've never seen white folks and colored folks getting together like that."

"Maybe not, but that doesn't mean they shouldn't, does it? One of the things I've learned these past few years is that the differences that separate us from other people are less important than the similarities that should bring us together. And one of the most contemptuous reasons for us to stay apart is the color of a person's skin.

"I've come to realize that I never intentionally avoided anyone who was a different color from me or attempted to do anything that was overtly discriminatory. However, I also never took it upon myself to get to know a person from a different race. That is the definition of discrimination. The fact that some people have to live in a different part of town, or eat in a different room at a restaurant, or ride in a different part of a bus—that's just wrong!

"So, Mom, I am grateful to God that I was chosen to get to know Larnell Williams and Frank Mack, and we call each other friends."

I watched as my parents exchanged looks; I knew I had given them a lot to think about. My dad changed the subject, so I followed his lead. We would talk more about this another day.

I was still catching up on my sleep, so I decided to call it an early night. The next day was Christmas Eve. After an early morning run and breakfast, I went downtown to the L.L. Stearns & Sons Department Store to do my Christmas shopping. Mom had once worked at the store that now covered a whole city block. It was supposed to have the best selection of goods and merchandise this side of Pittsburgh or Philadelphia. Given its size, I think that was a fair assessment.

I selected a necktie for my dad and a lace handkerchief for my mom, which the store boxed and giftwrapped for me. On impulse, I decided to buy three more handkerchiefs. I was pleased that I was now prepared for the gift-giving season.

I took my time walking over to the tea room to meet Rob. My mouth watered as I thought about the basket of freshly baked sticky buns the waitress always brought to your table.

They melted in your mouth, and the wait staff could never keep a basket filled. You can only imagine what a couple of hungry Army officers could do to that basket!

"Did you read that General Patton died Friday?" Rob asked as we sat down.

"Yes, I was sorry to hear it. Evidently, he experienced complications from an accident he had in Germany while we were heading back to the States. We owe him our lives. He covered our backs at the Kasserine Pass. I think a lot of us wouldn't be alive today if it weren't for him. I know some folks didn't much like him, but to me, he will always be a true hero."

Rob and I spent our lunch comparing notes on how our weekends had gone now that we were back home. We both had felt strange—and we admitted it was probably strange for our parents as well. We would all just have to settle into a new normal.

"But I don't know if I'm going to stay in Williamsport," I added. "I'm headed down to see Lizzie the end of the week, and I don't know what's going to happen there. I know she expects us to get married and settle in Richmond, but I don't know if that's the best place for us. What are you going to do, Rob?"

"I'm not completely sure either," he replied, "but for now I think I'll stay here. I've done all the traveling I want to do for a while. If I can find the right girl, I may just get married and start my own construction company here in town. In the meantime, I spoke to Harry Winter at church yesterday, and he told me there's an opening for me at Vallamont Planing Mill if I want it. I told him I'd stop by the day after Christmas to talk about it."

"I'm pretty sure there's something for me at Lundy Lumber as well," I said. "But I don't know if that's what I want to do. I've decided to hold off planning any next steps until after I've been to Richmond."

Though we weren't wearing our uniforms that day, our appearance still gave us away. Almost everyone in the restaurant thanked us for our service. When we were leaving, the man behind the cash register wouldn't let us pay for our meals, despite our protests.

I needed to make three more stops that afternoon. After picking up three small Christmas arrangements at the florist's, I went to visit the mothers of Doug Fessler, Rick Gordon, and Bill Martin.

"I was proud to serve with your son, ma'am," I told each grieving mother as I presented her with a gift in memory of her son. "If there is ever anything I can do for you, never hesitate to reach out to me."

---

[1] John 15:13 (ESV)

13

MONDAY EVENING, DECEMBER 24 – SATURDAY, DECEMBER 29, 1945

~

I decided to make one more visit—this one to Larnell's parents. The afternoon had disappeared, and it was now early evening. I knew they might be celebrating Christmas Eve with their family, and I didn't want to intrude, but I also didn't want to put off paying them a visit.

They lived on Locust Street, just around the corner from the Bethune-Douglass Community Center, named for educator Mary McCleod Bethune and author/activist Frederick Douglass. Though the facility was only about a half mile from my parents' home, it was an area of town in which I'd never spent any time.

When I walked onto the front porch of the Williamses' bungalow, I was immediately greeted by the sights, aromas, and sounds of the merriment of Christmas. A young woman who, based on Larnell's description, I was certain was his sister, Rebecca, answered the door. I could tell she was surprised to see me —a stranger on Christmas Eve—and a white stranger at that!

Mr. Williams joined her at the door and vigorously shook my hand.

"Major Fearsithe, Merry Christmas to you!" he joyously declared. "We didn't expect to see you tonight, but we are glad to have you. Please come in where it's warm and make yourself at home."

Their home was filled with what I assumed were family and friends. Suddenly, you could hear a pin drop as they all stopped talking and stared at me. Mr. Williams immediately filled the silence.

"Everyone, this is Larnell's friend, Major Fearsithe. They went through Officer Candidate School together and the major here helped save my boy's life."

The stares turned to smiles and nods of acceptance as people welcomed me and shook my hand.

"Please call me Bobby. Merry Christmas to you all!" I called out.

Mrs. Williams walked over and gave me the kind of hug that warms you all over.

"Welcome to our home, Bobby. We are so glad you are here!"

"I didn't mean to impose, Mrs. Williams. I can see you have a houseful, and I don't want to take you from your guests."

"Oh, these aren't guests, Bobby," she laughed, "these folks are family— some by blood, and some not. You're family, too, so don't go troubling yourself. And while we're at it, no one in my family calls me Mrs.

Williams. They call me Momma, and I expect you to do likewise —or else I'll be calling you Major Fearsithe!"

"Then Momma it is!" I replied with a grin. "But I can't stay long, I need to get back to the Christmas Eve party my parents are hosting."

"Stay as long as you like and know you're always welcome."

Before I realized it, I had been there about forty-five minutes, enjoying the anecdotes about Larnell from his younger days and about how much he enjoyed Christmas. I asked his parents if I could have a moment to speak with them before I left.

"I'm headed to Richmond for New Year's, so I plan to spend some time with Larnell," I told them. "If you have any cards, gifts, or anything else you would like me to deliver, I would be more than happy to do so.

"And Momma, I don't expect Larnell had much time for Christmas shopping this year. So I picked this up for him, because I know he would have done the same for me. Merry Christmas, Momma, from Larnell."

When she unwrapped that lace handkerchief, you would have thought it was the Hope Diamond. She wrapped her arms tightly around me and wept gently on my shoulder.

"I know Larnell will be glad to get home to you. In the meantime, I'll be sure and tell him you liked his gift," I said as I returned her embrace.

It began to snow as I walked back home. I had hated the snow when I was in Europe, but tonight was different. There's something about Christmas Eve, snow, and family that makes it all special.

My family's party was in full swing when I arrived home. My mom gave me a quizzical look, so I told her I'd explain later where I had been. While our guests told stories, sang carols, and enjoyed wonderful refreshments, I thought back to our Christmas Eve four years earlier.

I glanced around the room at some of the men I had served with—Rob, Donny, and Jack. I recognized families who had lost loved ones in the war. I identified others who had scrimped and sacrificed to support the effort.

I had been waiting the entire evening for the Marconi to play one particular song. When I heard the first few notes of "White Christmas," I walked over to my mother, took her hand, and turned our living room into our own personal dance floor. As we quietly floated around the room, I noticed our guests had tears in their eyes as they watched our special moment. We truly had something extra for which to be grateful this holiday season.

We really did have a white Christmas as nine inches of fresh snow fell during the night. Neighborhood kids enjoyed every moment—from snowball fights to sled rides to snowmen—before they retreated indoors for some hot chocolate and that memorable, once-a-year dinner.

The next morning, I headed to the local Buick dealership. The owner, Tommy Richardson, was a longtime friend of my dad's, and I was confident he would give me a good deal. I purchased a black, 1940 Buick Special for $600. It wasn't the smartest-looking car on the road, but it would get me where I was going. Tommy told me he had given me the soldier's discount, whatever that meant, but it seemed like a fair price.

On Thursday, I stopped by to see Mr. Lundy. The first thing he asked was if I was looking for a job. I told him I might be, but I wasn't sure. He promised to keep an opening for me.

"I need someone to head up my contractor sales operation," he said. "There haven't been any new homes built in Williamsport in four years. But with all you GIs coming back from the war and marrying your sweethearts, we're about to see a growth explosion unlike anything we've ever seen."

It did sound like a great opportunity, and I knew I would never find a better boss than Mr. Lundy.

"I'm headed to Richmond, Virginia, this weekend," I told him. "I should have a pretty good idea of what I'm going to do after that. I'll come by and give you my answer when I return."

I set out for Richmond at 8:00 a.m. Saturday. Lizzie was expecting me in time for dinner at 6:00 p.m., so I made sure to allow extra time for any unexpected emergencies. Mr. and Mrs. Williams had stopped by the day before with their care package for Larnell, so my trunk was full to capacity.

Traffic was light and the weather was mostly sunny as I made my way south. The Buick was a lot more comfortable than an Army jeep! I stopped at a diner for lunch once I crossed into Maryland.

I wasn't sure how much traffic I'd encounter when I passed through Washington, D.C., but apparently everyone had taken the weekend off from running the country and was enjoying their holiday at home. I momentarily considered taking a brief detour to take a driving tour around the White House and National Mall, but I decided not to risk the time. I made a mental note to do so on my trip back to Williamsport.

Not long after passing through our nation's capital, I came upon the Marine Corps Base in Quantico, Virginia. The Marines had helped save my bacon more than once during the war, and I was more than grateful to them. I realized the traffic wouldn't permit me to pull over and do a proper job of it, but I still took a moment to give a smart salute as I drove by.

The sun was just about to set as I arrived in Richmond. I knew I was in the former Capital of the Confederacy when I spotted street signs like J.E.B. Stuart Parkway and monuments honoring General Robert E. Lee and President Jefferson Davis.

The Dodd's home stood on the corner of Monument and Bellissimo Avenues in an affluent section of the city. I knew Lizzie's family was wealthy; she had never kept that a secret. Though my dad was a successful businessman and we lived comfortably, I would never have called us wealthy. However, as I parked my car in front of one of the grander, antebellum-style mansions on the avenue, I had no doubt as to the financial means of this family!

Though I was supposed to be a house guest for the weekend, I left my suitcase in the car in case they took one look at me and threw me out. I approached the door with the same butterflies I had felt that night Rob, Donny, and I reported to Sergeant O'Reilly in the latrine. It didn't help that the butler who greeted me bore a slight resemblance to the sergeant.

"Good evening, Major Fearsithe," the butler said in a deep baritone voice as he ushered me into the foyer. "My name is Cavendish. Welcome to the Dodd family home. They have been expecting you."

A familiar voice rang out behind me. "Yes, we have been expecting you, and I thought you would never arrive!"

Lizzie had obviously told her family how she felt about me because she clasped her arms around my neck and brought her lips to mine. So much for my apprehension!

"My family is in the parlor waiting to meet you," Lizzie said. "Give Cavendish your suitcase and he'll take it to your room." Not seeing my bag, she asked, "Bobby, where is your suitcase?"

"Oh, I must have left it in the car."

"Well, that's not an issue," she replied. "Give your key to Cavendish, and he'll retrieve it for you."

There was no turning back now! Lizzie led me into their beautifully appointed parlor where her parents and younger sister were seated.

"Mommy and Daddy, allow me to introduce you to Major Robert Fearsithe —but he will insist that you call him Bobby."

I extended my hand as Mrs. Dodd rose to greet me with a disarming smile and a gentle touch.

"Bobby, it is our great pleasure to finally meet you in person. I do believe that with all Elizabeth has told us, we feel we already know you. We are glad you are able to join us for this holiday weekend, and we hope you will make yourself at home."

"Thank you for including me in your plans and extending your kind hospitality," I replied. "It is a privilege to meet you, Mrs. Dodd."

Lizzie's father shook my hand saying, "Major, it is a distinct honor to meet one of our nation's decorated heroes from the war in Europe, and we welcome you into our home. I look forward to getting better acquainted."

"As do I, sir," I said as I returned his firm handshake. "Thank you for having me, but please do call me Bobby."

The remaining person in the room then spoke up, "Well, I will definitely call you Bobby! As you probably guessed, I am Elizabeth's sister, Anne, and I too have looked forward to your arrival—partly because you are all my sister has talked about since she returned from England," she added with a wink and a chuckle. "Hopefully, now we can get her to tell us more about her time in Europe."

"Well, if that's the case, Lizzie has definitely saved the more interesting news for last," I retorted as we shook hands. I noticed a surprised look on all three faces when I used the name Lizzie. The woman herself simply smiled at her family. Apparently, I had exclusive rights to that nickname.

"Bobby, you probably want to freshen up after your long drive," Mrs. Dodd suggested. "Elizabeth, why don't you show our guest to his room, and we'll plan to sit down for dinner in fifteen minutes."

As I climbed the stairs to my room, I noticed the remainder of the home was furnished as exquisitely as what I'd already seen. Christmas decorations adorned everything perfectly, neither too ostentatiously nor too sparingly. Lizzie's mother clearly had a flair.

"I can tell they like you," Lizzie said.

"Well, of course they do! What's not to like?" I teased.

"I see you grew in humility over these past several months in West Germany," Lizzie retorted.

When we headed down to the dining room, Cavendish approached me and asked, "Major Fearsithe, I couldn't help but notice all the goods in the boot of your car. Would you like me to bring those in?"

"Thanks for asking, Cavendish," I replied. "No, I will leave those in the car. They are for a friend I plan to visit tomorrow."

Lizzie gave me an inquisitive look, so I explained.

"Those are for Larnell from his family. I had a delightful time with them on Christmas Eve. I will tell you all about it later."

The meal was as perfect as the furnishings, featuring a deliciously prepared red snapper with steamed broccoli, sweet potato slices, and peach salad. I could tell my food palette was about to expand this weekend.

After dinner we returned to the parlor and continued talking well into the evening. I gave Mrs. Dodd and Lizzie the lace handkerchiefs I had bought them. They seemed pleased with their presents, though I regretted not having gifts for Anne and Mr. Dodd.

Lizzie's father was interested in talking about my work pursuits now that the war was over. Mrs. Dodd was mainly interesting in learning more about my family. Lizzie eventually announced good-naturedly, "Family, may I suggest we allow our guest to take a break from this evening's inter-rogation? We'll permit him to get some rest before we resume round two tomorrow."

Mrs. Dodd looked at me in horror. "Have we been that bad, Bobby? Please forgive us! Our daughter has a head start on getting acquainted with you, and we simply want to catch up. Thank you for humoring us tonight. We'll turn the tables tomorrow and let you ask all the questions."

She smiled at her daughter and asked, "Is that fair, Elizabeth?"

However, I replied first. "That is more than fair; but please know I enjoyed this evening. I want us all to be comfortable with one another, so feel free to ask me any question on your mind.

"Besides, your interrogation skills are nothing compared to those of the Nazis." Then I added with an impish grin, "They were close … but not quite!"

We enjoyed a good laugh before heading off to bed.

∾

14

SUNDAY, DECEMBER 30, 1945

~

I started the next day with an early morning run along Monument Avenue down around Stuart Circle and back. The temperature was moderate for December 30, making for an enjoyable run.

Along the way, I passed an impressive structure. The sign outside read:

FIRST BAPTIST CHURCH
PASTOR THEODORE F. ADAMS
11:00 A.M. SUNDAY

When I arrived back at the Dodd home, the cook, Esther, was busy in the kitchen preparing breakfast. I offered to make coffee, but she told me it was already done. I promptly realized she made a much better cup of coffee than I do.

Cavendish offered to take my coffee into the sunroom so I could enjoy reading the morning edition of the Richmond Times-Dispatch. Two headlines caught my eye:

```
2,600 U.S.-trained Dutch troops land in Jakarta,
   Indonesia, to help reimpose colonial rule
```

and

```
Koreans attack American soldiers in Seoul to
   protest five-year wait to restore Korean
                independence
```

Peace in the world was still quite fragile, and I feared that, to at least some degree, it always would be.

Lizzie joined me in the sunroom as I finished looking at the paper.

"I am told the major still rises well before the sun," she said. "I thought you knew this was a holiday weekend, which gives you permission to sleep a while longer."

"I decided to enjoy my holiday with a refreshing run and explore some of your neighborhood," I replied.

"Oh, you did!" Lizzie exclaimed. "And what did you discover?"

"There's an 11:00 a.m. worship service at that big church down the street. Do you want to go with me?"

"Yes, the First Baptist Church," Lizzie remarked. "My parents attend there on occasion, and I did when I was younger. We can go if you like."

"Yes, I would like for us to go together."

After another delicious meal, we got ready and headed to church. I was pleased that the entire family decided to join us. As we made our way to a pew, I noticed many in the congregation seemed to know the Dodd family. I assumed it was due to their social standing rather than their devoutness.

The service began with a rousing collection of familiar hymns. The building's acoustics seemed to make the music sound even more heavenly, and the choir's performance stirred my spirit. I had always enjoyed the humble musical offerings at Memorial Baptist Church back home, but these were the most celestial I had ever heard.

Reverend Adams's message was taken from the book of Ecclesiastes.

"In Ecclesiastes 4:9-12, we find wisdom that transcends time, revealing truths that are relevant to our lives today. We are reminded of the power of walking together in agreement.

"The author begins by stating, '*Two are better than one.*'[1] This simple truth holds immense significance. We are not meant to journey through life alone. We are social beings, created for fellowship and companionship. When we walk in unity with others, we experience the beauty of shared joys and sorrows. Our burdens become lighter, and our victories are more meaningful."

I looked over at Lizzie and smiled when she squeezed my hand.

"The passage goes on to highlight the practical benefits of companionship. '*If either of them falls down, one can help the other up.*' [2] As we know only too well, life is full of trials, and there are moments when we stumble and fall. But when we have someone walking alongside us, that companion can lift us up, offer support, and help us continue on our journey. This strengthens the bond between individuals and reinforces the idea that we are not alone in our struggles.

"Moreover, the author poignantly observes, '*But pity anyone who falls and has no one to help them up.*'[3] Loneliness is a bitter experience, magnified in moments of weakness or distress. Without the support of others, our burdens become heavier and our journey more difficult. So, we are challenged to extend a hand of compassion to those who are alone and become the friend they desperately need."

The pastor went on to talk about the coldness of life's trials and how the warmth of companionship is a source of comfort and strength. "*Also, if two lie down together, they will keep warm. But how can one keep warm alone?*"[4]

Lizzie smiled at me to communicate her complete agreement with the pastor on this point.

He continued his message with the example of a cord with three strands. "'*Though one may be overpowered, two can defend themselves. A cord of three strands is not quickly broken.*'[5] Together, we are stronger. When we stand in agreement, united in purpose and spirit, we become a formidable force against the challenges of life. Moreover, the reference to a cord of three strands reminds us of the importance of including God in our relationships. With God as the third strand, our agreement becomes unbreakable, rooted in divine love and wisdom.

"In conclusion, Ecclesiastes 4:9-12 teaches us the profound truth that agreement is essential for a fulfilling and meaningful life. As we walk together in agreement, supporting and uplifting one another, we experience the richness of companionship and the strength of solidarity. Let us, therefore, as we enter into this new year, seek to cultivate agreement in our relationships, knowing that together, we can overcome any obstacle that comes our way. Amen."

Reverend Adams greeted us at the door as we exited. Mr. Dodd introduced me as a guest of their family, and a war hero recently returned from Europe.

"Reverend, thank you for your challenging message from God's Word this morning," I said as we shook hands.

"Major, thank you for your heroic service for our country," he replied. "Your accent tells me you are not from around here, but I hope that will change and we will see more of you in the weeks to come."

I couldn't help but notice that he smiled at Lizzie as he made that last comment.

"And please be sure to bring this precious family with you when you return," he continued. "It has been far too long since the Dodds joined us on a Sunday morning. I am always so grateful when they do," he added sincerely.

The five of us chatted cordially as we walked at a leisurely pace back to the Dodd home.

"Mommy, if you don't mind, Bobby and I want to stroll for a few more minutes and enjoy this December sunshine. What time are you planning to have Sunday dinner?"

Lizzie assured her mother we would return ahead of schedule, so she and I continued our walk along the avenue while the others headed into the residence. I saw it as my opportunity to have the conversation with Lizzie that I knew I needed to have with her.

"Lizzie, what did you think of the pastor's message this morning?"

"I thought he was eloquent as usual," she replied, "and I couldn't help but wonder if he had prepared his message about companionship specifically for us. What did you think?"

"I thought his words were apropos as well—particularly when he talked about God being the third strand that makes the cord of relationship unbreakable. It caused me to wonder if God is the third strand in our relationship. For that to be the case, we both need to have a saving relationship with Him. I don't think He can be the third strand if only one of us does."

"Bobby, I know your relationship with God means a lot to you," Lizzie replied, "but I didn't know my belief in Him meant that much to you."

"It means everything to me, Lizzie. I believe the most important relationship I will ever have is with God. It's even more important than the relationship I will have with the one I one day marry.

"If my life partner doesn't feel the same way I do, we'll be out of alignment on everything else—our relationship, our future, and, most importantly, our faith. So, if you and I are going to move forward in this courtship, we've got to make sure we agree about what we believe about God. The apostle John wrote in the Bible: 'I write these things to you who believe in the name of the Son of God, that you may know that you have eternal life.' [6]

"When John writes that we must believe in Jesus, he's talking about a whole lot more than simply believing He exists. It means trusting Him completely with our lives and giving Him complete control.

"But I can't do that for you, and you can't do that for me. You can't choose to believe in God because I do. You have to do so because you love Him, trust Him, and know that apart from Him you are lost. You have to want it even if I'm not in the picture. Does that make sense?"

"I understand what you are saying, but I don't like where this conversation is headed," Lizzie answered. "Are you saying our relationship cannot advance if I'm not willing to surrender my life to God?"

"Lizzie, we'll be friends no matter what you decide," I replied. "You were my friend when I desperately needed one. But we can't consider the possibility of becoming husband and wife if we are not in the same place as far as God is concerned. And you can't decide to believe in God because of me. If you're going to choose to follow Jesus, you must choose because of you ... and because of Him."

"Bobby, this is not the conversation I imagined we were going to have on this stroll. I thought you were going to ask me to marry you. But instead, you're asking me to marry God! And Bobby, I'm not sure I'm ready to do that."

"I understand, Lizzie. And I'm not wanting you to decide right now. I will give you all the time and space you need to make a decision."

"I wish you had mentioned this earlier in our relationship, Bobby, particularly if this is so important to you. But I need to ask ... is there someone else?"

"No," I quickly replied. "You are the only woman I care about, and the only one I have ever considered marrying. But God has been reminding me—even through the message this morning—that if we don't settle this now, it could be disastrous down the road. And I don't want that to happen to either one of us. I love you too much."

"So where do we go from here?" Lizzie asked as a tear slid down her cheek.

"That's entirely up to you," I replied. "I want to do whatever makes you the most comfortable. I want to give you space, so I can pack my bag and leave now, or I can stay until Wednesday as we had planned."

"I know my parents planned to introduce you to all of their friends tomorrow night at their New Year's Eve party," Lizzie responded. "And I don't want to cast a pallor over their festivities. I'm prepared to continue on as we planned. Besides, who better for me to ask questions about God than you? Our walks will just have a different purpose than what I expected. Who knows, that may end up being a good thing."

I asked Lizzie if I could say a prayer, asking God to guide us in the decisions before us.

"Lord, we want only Your perfect plan, Your best, for both our lives," I prayed, "because I know You love both of us perfectly. Please open our ears and hearts to hear from You and know clearly what that is."

I was surprised when I heard Lizzie say softly, "Amen."

We returned to the Dodd home and enjoyed another delightful meal. Lizzie and I agreed not to mention anything to her family—neither of us wanted them to influence the decisions we were praying about.

After dinner, Lizzie and I went to McGuire General Hospital to see Larnell. As we drove over the James River, Lizzie explained that the hospital was a 1,785-bed facility. It was named in honor of the physician who had amputated Confederate General Stonewall Jackson's arm after the "friendly fire" wound that ultimately led to his death. I was beginning to understand that most everything in Richmond was named after someone or something that played a role in the Confederacy.

I was surprised to see that the hospital was a large compound consisting of sixty-nine individual structures. I was glad Lizzie was with me; otherwise,

I would have spent the rest of the day trying to find Larnell. She helped me locate a small wagon so I could deliver the gifts from his family.

I'm not sure which one of us was happier to see the other. Lizzie had told Larnell to expect my visit.

"Well, it's about time, major," Larnell said sarcastically. "It's half past three in the afternoon. I see you have transitioned back to the leisurely civilian life of sleeping your day away. I hope this trip didn't cause you to get out of bed too early!"

"Me?" I replied with a laugh. "Look who's still in his pajamas in bed, captain!"

I was glad his firm grip was returning as we shook hands.

"You are a sight for sore eyes, Larnell," I said. "You know I missed you by a day at Fairfield back in August. I arrived the day after you left."

"I know," he replied. "But you and I both know whom you were really coming to see," he added as he cast a smile and a glance at Lizzie.

"I needed to make sure she survived all the terrible treatment you and the other boys put her through," I countered in jest.

"Larnell knows better than that," Lizzie interjected. "He knows I am able to take care of myself just fine. They were putty in my hands."

Larnell responded with a laugh before asking me, "So what are all those boxes and envelopes you have in that wagon? Did you forget Christmas was last week?"

"No, I'm just Santa's deliveryman. These are all from your family."

"You met my family?"

"Your parents met me at the bus terminal when I arrived in Williamsport. And your mother gave me a great big hug. You haven't had a hug until you've been hugged by your mother."

"You've got that right!" Larnell nodded. "Did she tell you to call her Momma?"

"She sure did," I replied.

"How are my folks doing?" he asked.

"They're missing you. They can't wait until you get back home. Actually, that's true of your whole extended family and friends. I stopped by to see your parents on Christmas Eve and arrived in the middle of their holiday gathering. But everyone made me feel right at home, including Rebecca."

"You met my kid sister?" Larnell declared with delight. But I saw that twinge that told me he was missing his family and wishing he had been there. I decided to wait for another time to tell him about the handkerchief I had given his mother on his behalf.

"I'm sure you'll get to see them all real soon," I said. "So bring me up to date on how you are feeling and what the docs are telling you."

Lizzie excused herself to check on other patients so the two of us could have time alone to catch up. I could tell Larnell was gaining strength, plus the cosmetic surgeries he was undergoing had already made a significant improvement in his appearance. Yet, he would always bear a facial deformity to some degree.

"They expect I may be able to go home in a couple of months," he added. "I know I'll be ready for it, but I don't know if the folks at home will be ready for my appearance."

"They'll be ready!" I replied emphatically. But honestly, I was worried about how he would be received—not by his family, but by the rest of the world.

~

[1] Ecclesiastes 4:9 (NLT)

[2] Ecclesiastes 4:10 (NLT)

[3] Ecclesiastes 4:10 (NLT)

[4] Ecclesiastes 4:11 (NLT)

[5] Ecclesiastes 4:12 (NLT)

[6] 1 John 5:13 (ESV)

15

MONDAY, DECEMBER 31, 1945 – EARLY MORNING, TUESDAY, JANUARY 1, 1946

~

*M*r. Dodd surprised me at breakfast Monday morning with an invitation to tour his company, Dodd Manufacturing. I had only heard bits and pieces about the company from Lizzie, so I was interested in learning more about how the Dodds made their family fortune.

I followed him out to his burgundy 1946 Ford Super DeLuxe Tudor sedan and couldn't help but admire its impressive lines.

"It's one of the first 100 that Ford produced," Mr. Dodd said proudly. "Harry Truman received the first one to roll off Ford's new assembly line after they converted over for post-war production. I was able to get the first one in Richmond—to the envy of a number of my friends, I might add. It's a beauty isn't it?"

"What a swell car," I agreed. "Doesn't this have the new flathead V8 239 cubic inch engine?"

"You are correct," Mr. Dodd replied. "They tell me it has a top speed of seventy-eight miles per hour, but I haven't found a good place to test that out. Maybe you and I can find a spot some time. But major, if we're going to talk about cars, and I'm going to call you Bobby, then it's only right that you call me Arthur. Do we have a deal?"

"We have a deal, Arthur! Thanks for that courtesy."

"Well, I figure you probably commanded men older than I am during your time in Europe. Am I correct?"

"Yes, sir."

"I thought as much. In that case, it doesn't feel right that you and I speak so formally."

"Well, thank you again, Arthur. How far are your manufacturing facilities from your home?"

"Not too far, about four miles from here, along the north bank of the James River."

"If you don't mind my asking, how did the company get started?"

"No, I don't mind. In fact, I appreciate your asking. I am always glad to tell our story.

"It began with my great-grandfather, Howard William Dodd. He was born in Denbighshire in the north of Wales. As a young man, he worked construction for an engineer named Rhys Davies. In 1836, a group of Richmond businessmen set out to capitalize on the growing railroad boom here in the U.S. They hired Davies to come from Wales to build their facility, and he brought several of his iron workers with him, including my great-grandfather. He would have been about your age at the time. He jumped at the opportunity and never looked back.

"The crew constructed the facility, the iron works, and the rolling mills, naming it Tredegar Iron Works after Davies' hometown in Wales. However, soon after the foundry works opened in 1838, Davies died from stab wounds sustained in a fight with one of the local workmen.

"The owners turned management of the company over to a local civil engineer with whom my great-grandfather Howard and some of his fellow Welsh lads didn't see eye to eye.

"Tredegar was experiencing some fiscal challenges, so several of the financial partners sold their interest and reinvested the money in my great-grandfather's new enterprise. Thus, Dodd Iron Works was formed in 1841. There was enough steam locomotive and railroad business to go around, so both companies did very well through the 1850s.

"However, when the Southern states formed the Confederacy and declared war against the Union, President Jefferson Davis and his generals approached both companies about retooling their facilities to produce munitions for the Confederate Army. By then, Howard's son, Joseph, was running the company. He was responsible for two strategic decisions that led to the continued success of Dodd Iron Works.

"First, he wisely convinced President Davis and his generals that if both companies retooled to produce munitions, the Confederate States of America would be unable to supply and build the rail transportation it would need in place after the war. Joseph successfully negotiated for Tredegar to convert their manufacturing lines to munitions, and Dodd would continue to meet rail needs.

"When the South subsequently lost the war, the Union, of course, looked more favorably on the decision Joseph had made, and Dodd Iron Works continued to prosper while Tredegar worked to rebuild its standing and success.

"Joseph's second wise decision was transitioning the company from iron to steel ahead of the financial panic of 1873. That decision placed the company in a strong manufacturing position to meet increasing demand. Accordingly, Joseph renamed the company Dodd Manufacturing.

"Joseph's son Charles, who was my father, led our company to retool to supply munitions for World War I. After the war was over, he retooled in such a way that Dodd was able to meet the needs of its industrial customers as well as the demands of the peacetime military buildup here in the States.

"I have continued to follow that strategy since taking over the company five years ago following my father's death."

"Are you and Tredegar still competitors?" I asked.

"Sadly, Tredegar has failed to keep pace and rumors on the street are that they will soon close their doors," Arthur replied. Though we were in many ways competitors, I grieve for them, because our roots are so indelibly intertwined.

"By the way, you may have noticed that my middle initial is 'H' which stands for Howard. My father's and grandfather's middle names were also Howard. It has been a reminder to each of us that my great grandfather's grit and determination, together with his Welsh roots, are a part of each one of us."

As we pulled onto the company's property, it was obvious that everything was in full operation—even on New Year's Eve.

"We operate twenty-four hours a day, Bobby," Arthur remarked in answer to my quizzical expression. "Steel mills never shut down; it's too costly to start them back up. So we run four forty-two-hour shifts through the week, employing 1,500 workers."

We spent several hours touring the expansive facilities. I was quite impressed with two things: the efficiency and orderliness of the operations, and the respect and camaraderie Arthur enjoyed with every worker we encountered. He was obviously not a boss who remained in an ivory tower distant from his workers.

It was nearly 4:30 p.m. when Arthur said it was time for us to head back to the house.

"Myra and my daughters will think I got lost in my work again and took you down with me," he laughed. "It won't be good for either of us if we get back home after sunset. The ladies have made special preparations for our gathering this evening."

As we drove back to Monument Avenue, I was totally unprepared for Arthur's next comment.

"You may have noticed, Bobby, that Dodd Manufacturing has passed from father to son through four generations. But I have no son to carry on that tradition. So the marital choice of my daughters, particularly my eldest daughter, is of great importance to me—beyond the desire every father has for his daughter's happiness.

"I am seeking an heir, so I am looking at the man my daughter sets her sights on through both of those lenses. I will rely on her ability to choose the right husband, but I alone will choose the right successor. I believe you have the makings of an heir, but only Elizabeth knows if you have the right makings to be her husband. If you do, you will one day be blessed with two of my greatest possessions."

I was truly honored, not only by his words but also by his confidence in me to openly share those sentiments—and I told him so.

"It is in God's hands," I responded. "I believe He directs our steps. I know He has directed mine from my birth until this moment, and I trust Him to continue to do so. I have found there is no one better in whom I can place my trust."

"My faith in God is not as strong as yours," Arthur replied. "But I admire that in you. I think you could be a good influence on all our lives."

"Thank you, Arthur, and thank you for the time today. I enjoyed seeing your company's operations, but I especially enjoyed getting to know you a little better. Elizabeth has repeatedly told me what a great man you are, and after today, I would have to agree."

We pulled up in front of the house and caught sight of Lizzie standing at the door.

"Where have you two been?" she asked. "I was afraid you had kidnapped him, Daddy!"

"No, I didn't kidnap him," he replied sheepishly, "but I did get to know him a little better. And that's a good thing. I will now return him to your capable hands, Elizabeth."

"Bobby, I have so much to tell you, and you probably have a lot to tell me as well. Our guests will be arriving in about an hour, so you need to rest and we both need to get ready. But after we ring in 1946 tonight, we need to talk."

"I look forward to it," I replied. "And there is no one I would rather see the new year in with than you."

The evening was spectacular. Myra Dodd most definitely knows how to host a party. The food was superb; not one detail had been left to chance. I felt like I was being entertained in a palace. The guest list included the Virginia governor, the Honorable Colgate Darden, and his wife, Constance, the Richmond mayor, William Herbert, and a number of bank presidents and influential businessmen. Lizzie wasn't exaggerating when she said her father could introduce me into all the right circles.

At the family's request, I wore my dress uniform. Arthur insisted on introducing me as Major Robert Fearsithe of the U.S. Army's celebrated First Division. I knew appearances were very important in these circles. I also sensed that Arthur had already warmed to the idea of my becoming his future son-in-law—he appeared to be genuinely proud of me. I felt a pang of guilt when I considered his reaction if that didn't happen.

I breathed a sigh of relief when the party was over. I was most comfortable just being Bobby rather than Major Fearsithe. But I realized the same was true for the Dodds. It was obvious as they waved goodbye to the last of their guests that they were ready to just be themselves too. I was genuinely becoming drawn to the down-to-earth side of this family.

Lizzie and I changed into more comfortable clothes before we met in the sunroom for our conversation. We could see the bright waning crest of the moon clearly through the glass ceiling. Lizzie remarked that it appeared as if we were observing the thumbnail of God.

She wasted no time before launching into the conversation.

"Daddy tells me the two of you had an enjoyable time together today," she began. "I think he is quite keen on you."

"I like your father very much," I replied. "He has accomplished a lot and has much for which to be proud; yet, he remains gracious and humble. I know I could learn a great deal from him."

"Well, that brings me to the matter that stands between us," Lizzie said. "I decided that if my relationship with God—or should I say my lack of relationship—is that important to you, it should be that important to me. So this morning I pulled out the Bible I was given as a little girl in Sunday School. I had not opened it since I was young. But I thought if you were this serious about it, it wouldn't hurt me to look for myself."

What she did next surprised me. She pulled the Bible out of an oversized pocket in her jumper as she continued.

"I was going to start reading in Genesis, but then I remembered the verse you quoted me from 1 John 5. It took me a while to figure out that book was different from the Gospel of John, but eventually I found it. I read the verse you quoted:

'I write this to you who believe in the Son of God, so that you may know you have eternal life.'[1]

"But then I read the next two verses:

'And we can be confident that He will listen to us whenever we ask Him for anything in line with His will. And if we know He is listening when we make our requests, we can be sure that He will give us what we ask for.'[2]

"So I decided if I really wanted to know God—the way you know Him—shouldn't I be able to ask Him for that? I mean, wouldn't that be in line with His will? And if it is, couldn't I be certain He would give me what I was asking for?

"Bobby, I'm not a heathen. I've been to church and Sunday School, and I've heard what I considered more than my share of sermons. But do you know what I have never heard?"

"No, Lizzie, what's that?"

"I never heard what I believed was the voice of God," she answered. "But this morning when I asked Him that question, I heard His answer just as clearly as I heard you. And He said, 'Elizabeth, I've only been waiting for you to ask!'

"Bobby, He told me I've never known because I never asked! I didn't know because I didn't want to know. Then I remembered a picture that used to hang in my Sunday School class. It was a picture of Jesus standing at a door waiting for someone to open it. That was me, Bobby. I had never opened the door—even though I knew He was standing there."

I noticed a tear roll down Lizzie's cheek as she continued.

"My eye was drawn to the beginning of that same chapter, where I read:

'Everyone who believes that Jesus is the Christ has become a child of God. And everyone who loves the Father loves His children, too. We know we love God's children if we love God and obey His commandments. Loving God means keeping His commandments, and His commandments are not burdensome. For every child of God defeats this evil world, and we achieve this victory through our faith. And who can win this battle against the world? Only those who believe that Jesus is the Son of God.

'And Jesus Christ was revealed as God's Son by His baptism in water and by shedding His blood on the cross—not by water only, but by water and blood. And the Spirit, who is truth, confirms it with His testimony. So we have these three witnesses—the Spirit, the water, and the blood—and all three agree. Since we believe human testimony, surely we can believe the greater testimony that comes from God. And God has testified about His Son. All who believe in the Son of God know in their hearts that this testimony is true. Those who don't believe this are actually calling God a liar because they don't believe what God has testified about His Son.

'And this is what God has testified: He has given us eternal life, and this life is in His Son. Whoever has the Son has life; whoever does not have God's Son does not have life.'[3]

"By not believing, I was calling God a liar! By not believing, I was standing on the other side of that door, separated from God, when all He wanted me to do was believe in His Son. All I had to do was open the door and become His child."

Tears were now streaming down both our faces.

"So Bobby, there in my bedroom this morning, I opened that door, I believed in Jesus, and became a child of God. Not for you, but for me—because I know that is what God wanted me to do.

"Regardless of where you and I end up, Bobby, I wanted you to be the first to know. Because you're the one who pointed me to the One who is now the most important Person in my life!"

∼

---

[1] 1 John 5:13 (NLT)

[2] 1 John 5:14-15 (NLT)

[3] 1 John 5:1-12 (NLT)

16

THE REST OF THE DAY, TUESDAY, JANUARY 1 – THURSDAY JANUARY 3, 1946

⁓

*L*izzie and I stayed up most of the night talking about her newfound faith. She was giddy with excitement as she peppered me with questions about her relationship with God. We agreed she needed to tell her family about her decision.

Our conversation eventually turned to our relationship.

"Lizzie, I'm delighted about your decision to follow Christ! And now that it's no longer an obstacle for us to move forward, I also think we don't need to rush into anything. I believe we should ask the Lord to show us how He would have us proceed. Do you feel the same way?"

"I agree 100 percent! I think it's wise for us to seek God's guidance and listen for His voice."

Then we did something we had never done before. Together we got down on our knees and prayed, asking God to guide our steps.

It was a few minutes before sunrise when Lizzie and I finally got to bed. But we were both up after only a few hours of sleep so we could go visit our favorite hospital patient before noon. We shot the breeze with Larnell for a few minutes, then Lizzie left to check on her other patients.

"Did you open all the packages your family sent?" I asked.

"I sure did," Larnell answered. "They contained some of my favorite foods, new socks to keep my feet warm, plus cards and letters from prit' near everyone in my family filled with well wishes and prayers. There was even one from my momma thanking me for the lace handkerchief I gave her for Christmas. You wouldn't happen to know anything about that would you?"

"Well, sure I do!" I replied with a mischievous grin. "Don't you remember asking me to pick that up for you when we last saw each other in Fairfield? If not, it must be all those drugs they had you on."

"Must be," Larnell said smiling. "Well, thank you for doing that. I was feeling pretty awful that I hadn't sent her anything, but you covered my back. So let's talk about you. How did your New Year's Eve go with Elizabeth's family?"

"It was beyond anything I could have hoped for. First, Lizzie's father gave me a tour of his business, and I had a great time getting to know him."

"Was he checking you out as a future son-in-law?"

"Yes, he was, but I think we were checking each other out as to the type of man we are. He gets high marks from me. He would have fit right in with our OCS cohort. I think you would like him. And I believe I got a passing mark from him."

"Something tells me you got more than a passing mark. I'm happy for you."

"And most importantly," I added, "Lizzie surrendered her life to Jesus yesterday. We stayed up all night talking about the Lord and even prayed together for the first time. I've been on cloud nine ever since."

"Praise God!" Larnell declared. "I am so happy for her—and for you. That's wonderful news! So what does that mean for the future of your relationship?"

"We agreed we're not going to rush into anything."

"So, that means you're going to wait a day or two before you ask her to marry you?"

"Very funny," I replied. "No, I want her to come to Williamsport first and meet my folks, and we don't have that scheduled. Also, I need to decide what I'm going to do for a living. Mr. Lundy has offered me a good job that could turn into a career, but Arthur Dodd told me he would like me to come work with him if Lizzie and I decide to get married."

"How do you feel about that?"

"It would be a great opportunity. And like I said, I think he and I could become good friends—but I'm not sure. I always figured I'd build a career and raise a family in Williamsport."

"Well, God will show you," Larnell replied. "He always does."

"Larnell, how about you? Would you ever consider staying here in Richmond? If I decided to settle here, would you consider coming here to work with me? Fort Benning showed us we make a pretty good team."

"Yes, we do," he answered. "But there's quite a bit of difference between living in Williamsport, Pennsylvania, and living in Richmond, Virginia, for a person with my skin color. Plus, I'm not sure I'd want to leave my family. Like you, I always figured I would live out my days in Williamsport. But I am honored you would even consider asking me to come here to work with you."

"Well, the offer stands if you're interested," I said, "whether I end up in Williamsport or here. Together we'll either set the building material business on fire in Pennsylvania or the steel business in Virginia!"

We had talked for over an hour, and I could tell Larnell was getting tired.

"Well, I think it's time for me to go. I'll be heading out to Williamsport tomorrow. Is there anything you want me to carry back to your parents?"

Larnell reached over and pulled an envelope out of the bedside table. "Yes, I'd appreciate your delivering this to my parents if you don't mind."

"Mind? If you hadn't written them a note, I was going to write one—just so I had a reason to get another one of your mother's hugs!

"I'm pretty certain I'll be back here soon though," I continued. "Is there anything you'd like me to bring you back from Williamsport?"

"Yes! Bring me a ring of bologna from Waltman's Meats. They have a stall in the center of the Market House."

"I know Waltman's well," I replied. "And their ring bologna is my favorite too. It will be part of my next delivery! And I'll look forward to us going for a long walk the next time I'm here."

"Bobby, there was something else I read in my Bible yesterday that I wanted to ask you about," Lizzie said as we drove back to her home. "It was in Acts 2 where Peter preached to the crowd. It says one of them asked him, *'What should we do?'*[1] He tells the crowd, *'Repent of your sins, turn to God, and be baptized.'*[2]

"Yesterday I repented of my sins and turned to God. So based on what Peter said, I need to be baptized, right?"

"Yes, you do," I replied. "Baptism tells everyone that you have repented and believed. It's a public testimony of your salvation and a first step of obedience to Jesus."

"That's what I thought," Lizzie said. "Then I would like to get baptized while you're still here in Richmond. I think First Baptist has a midweek service tomorrow night, and I'm going to ask if I can be baptized then. I would really like you to be here for it. Would you be willing to stay over one more day and go back to Williamsport on Thursday?"

"I most definitely would!" I exclaimed enthusiastically. Lizzie wore the most radiant smile I had ever seen—exuding the joy of the Holy Spirit.

That evening at dinner, she announced her intentions to be baptized the following night and invited her family to attend.

"Don't you think you should make sure it's all right with the pastor before you plan it, Elizabeth?" Mrs. Dodd asked.

"I'm pretty certain it will be all right with him," Lizzie answered with confidence.

The next morning, I walked with her to the church where she was able to interrupt Pastor Adams' schedule to make her request. As she and I both expected, he was more than delighted to hear her news and honor her request.

"Elizabeth, I know the angels are rejoicing in heaven over your decision," the pastor said, "and so am I. I pray the rest of your family will one day follow your example."

We all attended the 6:30 p.m. service to witness Lizzie's baptism. Though her mother and father were genuinely happy for her, they obviously didn't quite understand what she was doing. But Lizzie and I both had a peace that the Lord was at work in their hearts as well.

Mrs. Dodd had delayed dinner until after the church service so we would not be hurried on my last night with them. As we were finishing our meal, Lizzie asked a question that caught all of us off guard.

"Mommy and Daddy, what would you think if I traveled to Williamsport tomorrow with Bobby to meet his family? I do not need to report back to the hospital until Monday. That way he would not have to travel home alone, and he and I could spend a few more days together. I could return home Sunday afternoon on the train."

I think Lizzie's parents could see that I, too, was surprised by her question, though I tried my best to hide it. However, I quickly warmed to the idea.

"Mr. and Mrs. Dodd, I think that is an excellent idea," I offered. "I know my parents would love to meet your daughter, and I would enjoy showing her around my hometown."

"It all seems a bit rushed to me," Mrs. Dodd expressed with concern. "Your parents haven't been given the opportunity to extend their own invitation; rather, my daughter is inviting herself. I do not like seeing them put in that position."

"I understand your concerns, Mrs. Dodd," I replied, "but if you are agreeable to the idea, I can telephone my parents and make sure they are receptive to the visit. Though, I can assure you with all confidence they will welcome her with open arms."

"What about you, Bobby?" Arthur asked. "I sensed you also were surprised by my daughter's announcement. Are you sure this is agreeable to you?"

"Absolutely," I replied with a sincere heart. "One of the many characteristics I find attractive in your daughter is her spontaneity. I believe most people could benefit from a little more spontaneity—at least, I know I could."

Mr. and Mrs. Dodd looked at each across the table, communicating with their eyes. It was Arthur who spoke first.

"Yes, Elizabeth, we are fine with you making this trip. You are a young woman capable of making your own decisions, just as you did this evening with your baptism. If your visit is okay with Bobby's parents, we see no reason why you should not go."

My mom picked up the phone on the first ring. Though surprised, she was delighted to hear from me. She shared the receiver with my dad so they could both hear the conversation.

"Mom, I am calling to see if would be all right for me to bring Lizzie home to stay with us for a few days."

"Oh, my Bobby! That's awfully sudden!"

However, when I told my parents what a wonderful visit I'd had in Richmond—and how much I really wanted them to meet Lizzie—they soon agreed and told me they would be looking forward to our arrival.

"And Mom, one more thing," I added before we hung up. "You will be delighted to hear that Lizzie surrendered her life to Christ on New Year's Eve and was baptized this evening. Jesus is now the first relationship in both our lives!" Though I couldn't see her face, I knew she was smiling.

One of the things the military teaches you is to be ready to go on a moment's notice, so Lizzie didn't require much time to pack her bag. After my early morning run and another of Esther's delicious breakfasts, Lizzie and I hit the road at eight o'clock.

It was another beautiful, sunny day—perfect for driving. However, this time the traffic congestion had returned, especially near Washington, D.C. Evidently, everyone was back at their desk running the country. Lizzie said we would have to arrange to travel to the nation's capital in April to enjoy the cherry blossoms.

"It is a marvelous sight!" she declared. The traffic situation prompted me to defer my planned drive around the White House until then as well.

We arrived in Williamsport in time for dinner. I could tell Mom had worked all day getting things ready for someone she considered a very special guest. And my sense of smell told me she had also prepared a scrumptious meal.

My mom and dad cordially welcomed Elizabeth into their home. By the time we had finished eating, the three of them were as comfortable as life-long friends. My dad even told Lizzie some of his favorite stories from his train trip to Portland, Oregon, in 1912.

One of his favorite tales was when a fellow traveler—the executive secretary of the Columbus, Ohio, publishing trade union—convinced my dad to get off the train in his fair city. He wanted my dad to meet two brothers, Harry and Robert Wolfe, who published The Columbus Dispatch and The Ohio State Journal. The two men spent the afternoon rolling out the red carpet for my father because the trade union secretary mistakenly assumed he was the son of a wealthy Philadelphia financier.

"Apparently the financier's son was traveling through that part of the country on behalf of his father to identify possible investment opportunities," my dad relayed. "And unbeknownst to me, he and I had stayed in the same hotel the night before in Pittsburgh. No one knew the wealthy financier's last name, so that prompted the mistaken identity when I mentioned where I had spent the night.

"I'll tell you, we all had an uncomfortable laugh when it became clear I was not the wealthy man's son, especially since my entire bankroll consisted of the less than $200 in my pocket. Needless to say, the two publishers wasted no time in bringing my VIP visit to a speedy conclusion."

My father concluded his story, just as he always did, with a chuckle. "But I ended up as the recipient of a spectacular meal as their guest for my efforts!"

Lizzie hung on every word of my father's stories and laughed in all the right places, which quickly endeared her to him.

When dinner was over, she helped my mom with the dishes. Though she had a serving staff in her parents' home, Lizzie pitched in as if that was what she was accustomed to doing. She demonstrated a genuine interest in my mom's stories as well, including the account of my parents' courtship. Lizzie drew insights out of my mother even I had never heard before.

But the conversation that brought the two women closest that night was sharing how they came to faith in Jesus. As I watched and listened, I realized there was no way I was not going to ask Lizzie to marry me! I was no longer running ahead of God; He had me running to keep up with Him!

---

(1) Acts 2:37 (NLT)

(2) Acts 2:38 (NLT)

17

FRIDAY, JANUARY 4 – SATURDAY, JANUARY 12, 1946

~

*L*ike half of the residents in Williamsport, Larnell's parents did not yet have a telephone, so there was no way to call and schedule a visit. So late Friday afternoon, Lizzie and I dropped in to see them unannounced.

Momma met us at the door wearing a brightly flowered apron and holding a wooden spoon. Between her appearance and the pleasing aroma that greeted us, there was no doubt she was cooking supper.

"Bobby, it's so good to see you!" she exclaimed, enveloping me in a big hug.

"And who's this beautiful young woman with you?" she asked as she greeted Lizzie with a welcoming smile.

"Momma, this is Elizabeth Dodd, the nurse who looked after Larnell all those months in Germany. In fact, she is still taking care of him in Richmond."

"Oh, thank You, Jesus! Miss Elizabeth, I can't thank you enough for what you've done for my boy," she cried out as she embraced Lizzie. "You are an angel sent by God! Larnell wrote about everything you've done for him.

"Gracious me, here I am making you stand out in the cold! Come on inside where it's warm. Oh honey, you're as pretty as Larnell said you were. Thank you for coming to see us."

A few minutes later, Clovis and Rebecca joined us, and Momma made introductions.

"How's Larnell?" Momma asked excitedly. "How is my boy?"

"He is doing well, Mrs. Williams," Lizzie assured her. "Given the severity of his injuries, he has come a long way in the past fourteen months. The surgeons did an excellent job of reconstructing his jaw and facial bone structure. The cosmetic surgeons also did a remarkable job of rebuilding his facial tissue. It won't be much longer now before he is released."

"Miss Elizbeth, we can never repay you for how much you've helped our boy. I know you and Bobby here have made a big difference in his recovery, and our family will always be obliged.

"When did you last see him, Bobby?"

"The three of us were together on Tuesday, Momma," I replied. "And he asked me to deliver this card to you."

"Oh, thank you Jesus!" she gasped as she took the envelope and brought it to her lips, kissing it repeatedly.

"Can you two stay for supper? We'd love to hear more about Larnell—and about what's happenin' between you two," she said with a twinkle in her eye.

"We would be delighted, if it's not an imposition," I replied.

"There's always room for family and friends at our table," Momma answered with a laugh, "and you two are family! Besides, Clovis and Rebecca say I cook for an army, so there's plenty of food. Supper'll be ready in a jiffy!"

Lizzie and I stayed late into the evening, enjoying good food and delightful conversation. Larnell's family told us all about his boyhood years—probably more than he would have liked us to hear! Lizzie shared about her family and her training as a nurse—both at the Medical College of Virginia in Richmond as well as in the Army Nursing Corps at the training center in Fort Meade, Maryland. They were quite impressed to hear she was a lieutenant in the Army.

"You know my Larnell was promoted to captain," Momma beamed. "We're so proud of him!"

But her face lit up most when Lizzie shared about her decision to become a Christian. Momma praised the Lord and gave Lizzie another bear hug.

Momma then turned to me and asked point blank, "So when are you two gettin' hitched, Bobby?"

"We're asking the Lord to show us His plans for our future," I assured her.

"Well, I'd say He's done already shown you," she added with a gentle laugh. "Now you just have to do somethin' about it!"

I was grateful when Rebecca spoke up and told her mother to quit meddling.

"Well, it's not meddling if it's plain as day," Momma countered.

Just before we left, Clovis took me aside and quietly asked me about Larnell's state of mind.

"He knows it's not going to be an easy road ahead," I replied. "He will be saddled with an obvious physical deformity for the rest of his life. And he will have to put up with chuckleheads poking fun at him—even though he was wounded defending their freedoms.

"We'll all need to be there to encourage him and walk with him each step of the way. But underneath, Larnell is still the same gifted, intelligent, and determined man. In the end, he will do well!"

On Saturday, I showed Lizzie around Williamsport—introducing her to some of my favorite spots when I was a teenager, as well as where I went to high school and college. I even took her by Lundy Lumber and introduced her to Mr. Lundy and my former coworkers. We spent a relaxing evening at home playing gin rummy with my parents, who entertained Lizzie with embarrassing stories from my childhood. I finally had to interrupt in order to protect a few of my secrets!

It was quite a contrast to the grander weekend Lizzie and I had spent in Richmond with her family—equally enjoyable, just in a different way. Before we said goodnight, I asked her if she could ever see herself living in Williamsport.

"It looks like a wonderful place to raise a family; everyone is so kind and friendly," she said. "And I believe a home is what you make of it. So, yes, I could see myself living here if it were with the man I love—and God shows us this is where He wants us."

At church the next morning, I realized this was the first Sunday morning service Lizzie had attended as a believer. I asked her what she thought after it was over.

"I never knew worship service could be so interesting and so exciting," she replied. "I always considered them long, boring, and dry; but this morning I realized that wasn't the case. I hadn't understood that the purpose of our singing, our praying, our giving—even our time together with one another —is an expression of worship to God. And the sermon is an opportunity to hear His truth. Today, I finally experienced real worship for the first time— with fresh eyes, fresh ears, and an open heart."

The time for Lizzie to board her train back to Richmond arrived much too soon. We had spent months together in Fairfield, but these past ten days had been different. I didn't want her to leave. I realized the war was now in my rearview mirror, and the future looked brighter than I could have imagined. I made up my mind what I needed to do.

"Lizzie, please ask your parents if I could come visit again this Friday. I have something I would like to discuss with your father."

As I watched her train pull out, I determined to hold our goodbye kiss and embrace in my heart until we were together again in five days.

As I loaded the trunk of my car early Friday morning, I knew It was probably the last time I'd cross the Mason-Dixon line for a while. If everything went according to plan this weekend, I would be making a permanent move to Richmond, Virginia. I would find an apartment to rent and hopefully prepare for the next chapter of my life. Though I hadn't asked Arthur for Lizzie's hand yet, I was reasonably confident of what he would say.

It had been a week of goodbyes. During my OSC training, we were taught the principle of "burning our boats." The idea, which comes from the ancient Greeks, is when you decide on an action, you must pursue it with an unwavering attitude of victory and commitment. When Grecian armies landed on their enemy's shore, the first thing the generals did was to give the order to "burn the boats," cutting off any avenue of retreat.

This week I had burned the boats. I had thanked Mr. Lundy for his gracious employment offer but told him I was accepting another position in manufacturing in Virginia.

"After meeting Elizabeth, I must say that doesn't come as much of a surprise," Mr. Lundy said with a grin. He kindly assured me that if things didn't work out, I would always have a job at Lundy's. I thanked him again and told him how grateful I was for his investment in me over the years.

It was particularly hard to say goodbye to Rob and Donny. I wished them well in their respective ventures and told them to stay in touch.

The most difficult farewell was with my parents. But having spent the past few years an ocean away, the eight-hour car ride to Richmond didn't seem all that far. And, of course, we would still visit regularly. They had fallen in love with Lizzie and approved of the decision I was making.

"You're not crossing the country on a train," my dad said, "and you're not abandoning your family—you are stepping out on a God-given pursuit. Son, please know our prayers and support are with you on this journey ... as well as our love."

Even though I ran into some heavy traffic near Washington, D.C., I still made it to Richmond in time for dinner. As I entered the city limits, however, it felt different this time. I was excited but also a little anxious at the same time. The butterflies in my stomach reminded me of the day my unit approached the French African coast. There may not be any bullets flying around now, but I knew the days ahead would not be without challenges.

Lizzie beat Cavendish to the door to greet me, but I also received a warm welcome from her family. Arthur acknowledged his receipt of my message through Lizzie and suggested the two of us meet following dinner. That suited me just fine, because I had no interest in putting it off.

He was not at all surprised by the topic of our meeting. He even told me that he and Mrs. Dodd had discussed the possibility of his daughter marrying me.

"Myra and I believe the two of you are a perfect match," Arthur confided. "Your strengths complement one another. In the short while we have seen you together, we believe you are better together than you are apart. We see a strength in you that we believe will sustain you through the difficult days of marriage—as well as the joyous ones.

"I told you earlier that the man who marries Elizabeth must be prepared to follow in my footsteps at Dodd Manufacturing. I have no doubt you are well suited for that role as well. Let me hastily add, though, it will not be given to you on a silver platter; you will need to earn it. But I have no doubt you will do so in a way that brings me great pride.

"So, Bobby, please know you have Myra's and my blessing with our affection and a pledge of our complete support."

"Thank you for that, Arthur," I replied. "And please know that as I propose to your daughter, I not only pledge my undying love and support to her, but also my undying affection and support for the two of you."

When we exited the study, Lizzie, her mother, and her sister were standing there waiting for us.

"Did you gentlemen have a good conversation?" Lizzie quizzed us, as all three women stared at us intently.

"Yes, we did, Elizabeth," Arthur replied. "It was the kind of good conversation men enjoy having with each other. We came to the same conclusion that we expect the Washington Redskins to redeem their loss from this past year and come back to win next year's NFL Championship Game. Isn't that right, Bobby?"

"By all means, Arthur!"

∾

I knew I couldn't keep Lizzie waiting. The next morning we awoke to springlike temperatures and sunny skies. After my early morning run and breakfast, I suggested we pack a picnic lunch and enjoy the grounds of the Maymont Estate. Lizzie had pointed out the historic landmark during my previous visit. Esther prepared a delectable picnic basket for us, and we set out to enjoy the day.

Prior to leaving Williamsport, I had told my parents I planned to propose to Lizzie, and they had given me their blessing. But I was completely taken by surprise when my father presented me with a red velvet box containing the beautiful diamond engagement ring my grandfather had given my grandmother. The stone and setting were exquisite, and the ring still sparkled as brightly as it must have on the day of their engagement. I was deeply touched and honored to present that family keepsake to Lizzie.

"Maymont," Lizzie explained as we drove to the park, "was the 100-acre Victorian country estate of James and Sallie May Dooley. In 1886, Mrs. Dooley led the effort to transform the rough pastureland along the north shore of the James River into a showplace. The end result rivals the lavish estates that sprang up during that era.

"The Romanesque-style mansion was finally completed in 1893, and Mrs. Dooley spent the next three decades filling it with treasures from around the world. She also established Maymont's magnificent gardens and land-scape as a tribute to her and her husband's love for one another.

"When the Dooleys died in the 1920s they left no heirs, so Maymont was bequeathed to the city of Richmond. The estate and grounds were opened as a public park and museum six months after Mrs. Dooley's death.

"A whole generation of Richmonders has grown up as recipients of the Dooleys' generosity. My mother often took Anne and me there in the cooler summer days for a picnic lunch and a romp in the park. I hope to do so with my children one day."

When we arrived at the park, we found a somewhat secluded spot over-looking the river. After feasting on Esther's lunch, I knelt on one knee before Lizzie.

My words may not have been the most poetic, but the surroundings were lovely, and the sentiment was from my heart. I told her she would always be the most important person in my life, second only to Jesus—and I would expect nothing less from her.

She was genuinely touched by the origins of the engagement ring I displayed in the red velvet ring box. I stared into her eyes as I awaited a response from the woman I knew God had created just for me. Gratefully, she did not keep me waiting long for her answer!

18

SUNDAY, JANUARY 13 – FRIDAY, FEBRUARY 22, 1946

∾

*A*fter Sunday worship service at First Baptist Church and brunch at the Dodds' home, Lizzie took me to see a house her family owned in the Fan District of Richmond. The district—so named because the streets are arranged in a fan shape—featured a vibrant atmosphere with tree-lined streets, posh shops, and fashionable restaurants. The area appealed to young professionals and up-and-comers seeking a mixture of urban convenience and neighborhood charm.

Arthur had purchased this Edwardian-style home, along with several others in the district, as an investment during the war. The prior tenant had recently moved, and Arthur told me the timing was providential. He would lease the home to me and I could move in immediately.

"Bobby, why don't you take the next two days to get situated in your new home?" Arthur suggested. "We can make Wednesday your first official day in the office."

I quickly agreed, then offered up a quick prayer of thanks that all the details surrounding my move to Richmond had been navigated so easily.

Since this would also be Lizzie's home once we married, I wanted to make certain she liked it too. Her eyes lit up as soon as she saw it. The rooms were light and airy with elegant but relaxed furnishings. We were pleased to find several rooms were already furnished. Plus, the wall colors of pastel blues and greens were Lizzie's favorite colors. Perfect!

Our wedding was the main topic of conversation around the evening dinner table. I had no idea how much was involved with planning nuptials! We needed to decide the time and place for our wedding, formulate a guest list, choose colors and flowers, the wedding party, and the list of details stretched on and on. Then Mrs. Dodd mentioned we must choose a time and place for our engagement party. I didn't even know there was such an event!

Arthur and I were keenly aware we were not the decision-makers on these subjects—and I had less say-so than Arthur. After all, he would be underwriting the soirées. So the two of us wisely remained silent while the ladies discussed plans. By the time the evening was over, our engagement party was set to take place in the Dodd home on Saturday, March 2.

Lizzie was adamant she did not want to wait any longer than June for the wedding, though Myra felt that was too short of an engagement. In the battle of wills between the two Dodd women, Lizzie won the day. Our wedding would take place sometime in June, subject to the availability of suitable ceremony and reception venues.

I smiled to myself as I watched the exchange between Lizzie and her mother. Lizzie and I had disagreed with one another on several occasions —enough for me to know I would always choose her as my debate partner!

After the engagement party was settled, I changed the subject and asked a question about an upcoming holiday.

"One of you mentioned a gala ball taking place this Friday as part of the state holiday observance. What holiday is it?"

"It is Lee-Jackson Day," Arthur replied. "Though it is observed in several states, it is only a state holiday in the Commonwealth of Virginia. We commemorate the contributions General Robert E. Lee and General Thomas 'Stonewall' Jackson made to our great nation and commonwealth as educators, leaders, and military strategists."

"I have never heard of the holiday," I said. "How long has it been observed?"

"It was instituted over fifty years ago by a Virginia governor, the Honorable Fitzhugh Lee, who also served as an officer in the Confederate army. The governor happened to be a nephew of General Lee," Arthur answered.

"We celebrate the day with a wreath-laying ceremony at Hollywood Cemetery—which is where President James Monroe is buried—with military honors, parades, and regional events around the commonwealth. Festivities conclude with a gala ball held here in Richmond at the Jefferson Hotel," Lizzie explained. "And you probably guessed the hotel is named in honor of Virginia's son, President Thomas Jefferson."

The holiday was a reminder that I was now living south of the Mason-Dixon line. I was beginning to realize how Virginians—and Richmonders, in particular—continued to embrace their Confederate heritage, even eighty years after the war. I wasn't quite sure where the Dodd family stood on all of this, though Lizzie told me we would be expected to attend the ball.

Over the next couple of days, Lizzie helped me find a housekeeper who would come two days a week. She also helped me stock up on a few grocery essentials. I didn't need much since I would continue taking most of my meals at the Dodd home, at least until Lizzie and I were married. Monday was the first night in my new home, which meant Tuesday's early morning run was along a new route through William Byrd Park.

I took advantage of this last day before work started to visit Larnell. I'm not sure if he was happier to see me or the ring bologna I brought.

"Do you have the strength to walk around the grounds?" I asked.

"I was just about to ask you the same question," Larnell replied with a grin. "Try to keep up with me!"

I was glad to see how much his strength had increased in the past week. We walked for an hour, stopping only once to rest. I caught him up on all the news since we had last been together—including my marriage proposal.

"I tried to warn Nurse Dodd about you," he said in a mock stern voice. "But if she accepted your proposal, that means she completely ignored my advice!" We both had a good laugh, and it felt like old times again.

By the time we returned to Larnell's room, it was obvious he needed to rest. I promised him I would be back during the weekend. I looked around the campus for Lizzie, but she was involved treating a patient, so I left her a note saying I'd see her later that evening.

At five minutes before eight o'clock Wednesday morning, I met Arthur at the offices of Dodd Manufacturing. My father and the U.S. Army had taught me if I wasn't at least five minutes early, I was late.

I spent my first day in the executive offices with Arthur but learned that was temporary. Arthur outlined my schedule for the next six months.

"For at least the next two months," he began, "you will work under the supervision of our head of manufacturing, Thomas Seymore. Your first few weeks will be spent as an apprentice worker in the foundry. So leave your good clothing at home for a while. Come dressed in your overalls, work shirt, and boots. Thomas will give you a list of everything you'll need.

"You will operate at the various work stations in the foundry until you have mastered each one. That is why I said at least two months; the time schedule depends on how quickly you master each skill.

"After that, you will report to the transportation section, followed by purchasing and inventory, product development, and quality control. Once you have completed the overall manufacturing orientation, you will move to your assignments in sales, administration, and accounting, successively.

"Beginning when I was just a lad, I worked in every position in the company. My father told me—and I wholeheartedly agree—there is no better way to learn the inner workings of this business. And I've come to realize the best boss is the one capable of doing any job in his company. I believe employees respect that in a leader. I have no doubt that if you apply yourself the same way you did in the Army, you will do well here.

"Unless you have any questions, Bobby, I will ask my secretary, Miss Hughes, to take you to our personnel office so you can complete the necessary paperwork. From there you'll be directed to Mr. Seymore, who will begin your introduction to manufacturing for the balance of the day.

"Do you have any questions for me?"

"No, you have laid it out quite well," I replied. "I look forward to meeting with you back here in six months!" I added with a grin.

My first few days at Dodd Manufacturing reminded me of my days in basic training. I didn't know anything, and each respective trainer took advantage of pointing that out, just as Sergeant O'Reilly had done. But as the days turned into weeks, my understanding of the most minute aspects of the business began to grow.

Arthur often quizzed me at family meals to glean how much I had learned. His questions most often were about policies and procedures of the section I was working in. Soon I was able to anticipate his questions and answer them with complete accuracy. However, one day I asked a question that caught him off guard—at least momentarily.

"Arthur, why are you resisting converting your manufacturing process over to the BOF (basic oxygen furnace) technologies being embraced in Europe and Japan?"

He hesitated a moment, then responded. "We are not convinced the benefits merit the capital investment required. It is one thing for plants that were completely destroyed by the war to employ this new technology as they rebuild from scratch. But it's quite another for companies like ours, that have a significant investment in the proven Bessemer air blast process, to convert."

"There is no question it would require a substantial investment to retool," I agreed, "but my concern is whether Dodd Manufacturing and others here in the U.S. will be left behind in the competitive race. It is that kind of short-sighted thinking, as you pointed out to me, that now finds Tredegar struggling to keep its doors open."

"There is no question, Bobby," Arthur countered with a polite smile, "that you are grasping both the micro and the macro strategies used in our business plan. I look forward to exploring these discussions further once you have completed your 'basic training.'"

February 22 was a special day—not only because it was my twenty-fourth birthday, but also because Larnell was being released from the hospital. I arranged to get off work a few hours early so I could pick him up from the hospital.

The doctors wanted Larnell to remain in Richmond for several weeks so they could monitor his progress. I insisted that he stay with me until the doctors released him.

"It will be like our days as roommates at Fort Benning," I told him.

"Are you sure it's all right if I stay with you?" Larnell asked.

"Of course, it's okay! It's my home, you are my friend, and I have the space."

We didn't mention it again.

When I had run the idea by Lizzie a couple of weeks before Larnell's release, she had given me a curious look. However, she didn't say anything, and I saw no need to pursue it further.

Larnell reminded me of a new puppy on his first automobile ride as we drove off hospital grounds. Even though the temperature was cool, he rolled down his window and hung his head out so he could feel the air blowing on his face. It was his first time away from the hospital since he had arrived in Richmond in August. And it was his first time not being under medical care since he was wounded sixteen months earlier.

He didn't say much, he just kept turning his head to take in all the sights.

"What do you think of Richmond so far, Larnell?" I asked. "Does it look much like Williamsport to you?"

"Parts of it do," he said, "but parts of it sure don't."

I drove him down Main Street so he could see the streetcars and automobiles jockeying for position. It didn't help that it was late Friday afternoon, and everyone was making their way home for the weekend. He just shook his head and laughed at the chaotic sight.

When I parked the car in front of my house, I almost laughed at Larnell's reaction.

"Bobby, is this your house?" he asked in amazement.

"Well, I am renting it for now," I replied. "Lizzie's father actually owns it. I can't afford to buy one like this just yet, but I plan to in the near future. Let's get you settled."

Larnell slowly got out of the car and up the stairs. The doctors had cautioned him to maneuver carefully so he wouldn't fall and reinjure his healing bones and skin.

He seemed to be even more impressed with the interior of the house.

"Are you sure you're not trespassing in this house, major?" he asked with a sheepish grin. "I just want to be sure no one is going to knock on the door in the middle of the night and tell us to get out of here!"

After I showed him to his room, I told him to make himself at home.

"Captain, you are neither my patient nor my guest; you are my roommate. Put away whatever you get out, clean up whatever you mess up, and help yourself to whatever is in the refrigerator—which isn't much. We can pick up some things you like at the grocery store tomorrow."

Lizzie had surprised me a few days earlier with the news that her parents had planned a party to celebrate my birthday with the family and a few friends.

"Do you feel up to coming to my birthday party tonight?"

"Are you sure I'm invited?" Larnell asked, a frown creasing his forehead.

"I know Lizzie didn't give you an invitation, but she didn't know you were going to be released today," I replied. "Of course, you're invited. It is a gathering of family and a few friends—and you qualify on both fronts!"

"I actually feel pretty good and would enjoy being out among other people," Larnell responded. "Do you think they'll be put off by the way my face looks?"

"No, I'll just tell them you're much better looking now than when I first met you," I replied with a laugh. "We're supposed to be at the Dodds' house at 1800 hours, so go ahead and rest until then. It's a dressy affair, so wear your dress uniform. Lizzie requested I do the same. We'll go shopping tomorrow so you can buy some new duds."

Larnell's reaction to seeing my home was nothing compared to his astonishment when we pulled up in front of the Dodd home. But to his credit, he walked up the front stairs as if he had been there many times before. Cavendish opened the door before I even knocked.

"Good evening, Major Fearsithe, and please allow me to wish you a happy birthday," Cavendish said before he turned to my companion.

"Cavendish, allow me to introduce you to Captain Larnell Williams," I said. "He is one of my dearest friends and a decorated war hero. He will be joining us tonight."

"Good evening, Captain Williams," he said somberly as he opened the door wider. "Welcome to the Dodd home."

19

FRIDAY, FEBRUARY 22 – SATURDAY
MORNING, FEBRUARY 23, 1946

～

*L*izzie noticed our arrival and immediately came over to greet us. I could tell she was surprised to see Larnell.

"Look at you two handsome gentlemen in your uniforms!" she declared, not missing a beat. "Tonight we will celebrate the birthday of one war hero and the release from the hospital of the other."

After giving us both a peck on the cheek, Lizzie asked Cavendish to add another table setting. We then followed her to the parlor where the guests were waiting.

Lizzie grasped the handles of the closed parlor doors and pushed them open with a flair. She stepped aside as people shouted, "Surprise!" followed by thunderous applause. But as Larnell and I walked into the room, the clapping abruptly stopped.

Lizzie immediately spoke up. "Father, Mother, and distinguished guests, please allow me to introduce my fiancé, Major Robert Fearsithe, whom many of you already know. With him is Captain Larnell Williams, a highly decorated war hero who was just released from McGuire General Hospital today after prolonged treatment for injuries he sustained in the war.

"Please join me again in thanking both of these brave men for their sacrifice and service."

The applause was somewhat more subdued than the first time. One by one those in the room approached us to express their polite, but reserved, greetings, starting with Arthur and Myra. They extended their good wishes to me for my birthday and expressed their gratitude to Larnell for his service. However, it was all quite cold and impersonal.

The Dodds then introduced the guests, starting with U.S. Senator Harry Byrd and his wife, Anne. Senator Byrd was well known on a national level for having led the opposition to Franklin D. Roosevelt's legislative agenda in the Senate. Even I knew who he was! The Dodds had joked at the dinner table one evening that nothing happened in Virginia politically that Senator Byrd did not first approve.

"Gentlemen, it is a pleasure to make the acquaintance of two war heroes such as yourselves. Major, I understand you served in the First Division under the command of my good friend, General Omar Bradley. You and your division did us proud, even under the questionable leadership of Field Marshal Monty Montgomery on Omaha Beach."

"Robert was wounded on Omaha Beach, Harry," Arthur interrupted.

"Thank you, son, for your bravery," the senator continued. "The heroic efforts of all you boys that day changed the course of the war and brought it to a much quicker conclusion."

Then he addressed Larnell. "Captain, I imagine you served in the Ninety-Second Infantry Division. Where were you injured?"

"During the attack on the Ligurian coast, sir," Larnell replied.

"I never thought it was fair to throw you boys into that fray that late in the war," the senator remarked. "You were untrained and untried. You were truly at a disadvantage. But thank you for your bravery."

The senator then turned to Lizzie's parents. "Arthur and Myra, thank you for this memorable opportunity to meet these fine heroes, but Anne and I need to skedaddle to another engagement. You know how politics can be. But thank you for inviting us—and Robert, happy birthday to you," he added, nodding at me. He and his wife hastily left the room.

Newly inaugurated Governor William Tuck and his wife Eva followed right behind the Byrds. The governor's remarks sounded very similar to Senator Byrd's, with the exception that he did not indicate an acquaintance with General Bradley. Coincidentally, they too feigned to have another unexpected engagement and left in a hurry.

Several others, also holding political offices, though in lesser stations, in what I soon learned was called the Byrd Organization—a political machine that wielded power and influence over Virginia government—followed the example set by the first two couples. However, a few guests stayed for the remainder of the evening including the Reverend Adams and his wife, Esther; Thomas Seymore from Dodd Manufacturing and his wife, Abigail; a couple of young Dodd executives, and a few bankers and their wives.

The serving staff unobtrusively adjusted the seating arrangements to cover the fact that almost half the crowd had just exited. The remaining guests attempted to ignore the elephant in the room by making a valiant effort to act as if nothing unusual had just occurred.

We all tried to enjoy the delicious meal Esther had prepared. She even baked one of my favorite desserts—peanut butter pie—in my honor. But despite everyone's attempts to carry on, the exodus had cast a pallor on the evening.

Not surprisingly, festivities concluded early. Larnell and I soon found ourselves alone with the Dodd family, who were cordial but not very talkative. After Lizzie and I arranged to meet the next morning to talk about the wedding, Larnell and I excused ourselves and headed home.

"I'm so sorry that my presence dampened your birthday celebration, Bobby," Larnell said as we drove.

"What do you have to be sorry about?"

"I should have known better than to come along with you, particularly uninvited," he said, his voice filled with regret. "That probably wouldn't have gone well in Williamsport, let alone in the capital of the Confederacy. I don't think you've heard the last of this, Bobby. I'm sure your future in-laws will have plenty to say. You put them in a tough spot. Make sure you tell them I'm staying with you. I don't think they're going to be too pleased about that either.

"Let's face it, Bobby, the world isn't ready for integration. Fort Benning showed us that! Some of those guys were never going to change no matter what we did. And people like Senator Byrd have made it their life's work to prevent it from taking place."

When I arrived at the Dodd home the next morning, Lizzie told me we needed to have a conversation with her father before we discussed wedding plans. He was waiting for us in his den.

"Bobby, I planned on having this conversation just between the two of us," Arthur began, "but Elizabeth insisted I include her. I hope you realize you put us all in a very difficult situation last evening. But I don't think you fully comprehend the extent of what it may have cost us.

"Our reputations, our standing in this community built over generations, our influence, and our political alliances have all been placed in jeopardy. Dodd Manufacturing itself now stands on the precipice of collapse because of your lack of judgment.

"What got into your head to think you could bring a colored man into our home as a guest? I know the two of you are Army buddies and that he risked his life in the war and paid a terrible price. I also know you and Elizabeth are in many ways responsible for saving his life. I applaud your humanity and compassion.

"But none of that changes the fact that he is a Negro, and this is Richmond, Virginia. Though the war over slavery and the South's view of coloreds may have been lost on the battlefield, it is still being fought in the political hallways and boardrooms throughout this Commonwealth.

"We invited Senator Byrd and the other members of his organization to your birthday party to introduce you to the inner circle that makes Virginia work. I built you up as a hero and leader of the next generation who will inspire great things in the future. They had expressed an interest in meeting you, and I thought there would be no better place than a simple social gathering to celebrate your twenty-fourth birthday.

"But in my wildest dreams I never imagined you would do something so foolhardy, so obtuse, and so insensitive to the conventions of this family, this city, and I daresay, this country. Are you totally unaware of the accepted manner in which whites and coloreds interact? Or is it so different in Pennsylvania?

"This morning I also learned that Captain Williams is staying in your home. I presume he is not a household servant. Are you not aware that colored people, other than servants, are not permitted to live in the Fan District? I am told several neighbors are planning to petition the local police to have him removed—by force, if necessary. I fear that will trigger an action to have you evicted from the home for failure to maintain proper housing standards.

"I must also point out that so far this morning, Myra has received no less than ten regrets from invitees to next Saturday's engagement party—all who previously had confirmed their attendance. We expect more regrets as news of last evening travels further ... which I assure you, it will!

"Are you beginning to understand the ramifications of your actions last evening?"

I looked over at Lizzie's stoic expression and honestly could not tell what she was thinking. Was she ready to call off our engagement?

"Arthur, I am greatly saddened by all you have told me," I began. "It grieves me that my actions have sullied the good name and reputation of your family. You and your wife have treated me like a son from the first day we met. You also have done everything possible to give me great advantages as I begin the next chapter of my life—professionally and otherwise.

"And my heart is broken that anything I have done caused pain to my precious Lizzie. I know every woman dreams of having the perfect wedding day and all the events surrounding it. To learn that our engagement party has been spoiled by what is seen as my 'moral failing' is distressing.

"But the thought that my actions might cause the downfall of a business enterprise that has been a giant in this community for four generations, injuring you and every person in your employ, is a consequence I am unable to abide.

"So, Arthur, what can I do? What action will place the blame solely on me and not negatively impact your lives? Surely, your reputations can withstand the momentary lapse in judgment of welcoming me into your home. What must be done to distance you from this incident?"

Arthur hesitated for a moment before answering.

"I wondered if you would try to justify your actions," he began. "I wondered if you might cite the great price Captain Williams paid in defense of the freedoms of the very people who are disparaging him because of the color of his skin. I even considered my own feelings on that point and contemplated what I would be prepared to forfeit in defense of his personal freedoms.

"But instead, you have spoken only of the harm this has caused me and my family. You demonstrated the same selflessness that made you stand head and shoulders above your comrades on the battlefield. I believe it will continue to serve you well throughout your lifetime.

"I admire you for that, Bobby, I really do. I can only hope to one day be that courageous and selfless. Unfortunately, I am not that man today. The implications of what has been set in motion are beyond what I can allow my family or my business to suffer.

"So, this is what must be done. Today we will announce publicly that you and Elizabeth have called off your engagement. We will give no reason for it ending. The same people who are expressing their displeasure will know the reason.

"As of now, you are no longer employed by Dodd Manufacturing. I will make a simple statement Monday that you and I came to a mutual agreement over the weekend resulting in your resignation.

"I also need you to vacate the home you're renting by Monday. I assume you will return to your parents' home in Williamsport. Suitable accommodations are available in the colored parts of town where Captain Williams can reside while he completes his treatment here in Richmond. I will underwrite the cost of those accommodations as an expression of my gratitude for his heroic service.

"Lastly, I will have Elizabeth arrange to be taken off the captain's case at the hospital so they no longer have any contact with one another.

"Bobby and Elizabeth, is my plan acceptable to the two of you?"

I glanced over at Elizabeth who remained silent, so I decided to proceed.

"Arthur, you hereby have my resignation from Dodd Manufacturing to communicate as you see fit. Also, I will vacate the home in the Fan District no later than Monday, once I know Larnell has acquired alternate lodging. As for your offer to pay for it, I will leave that matter entirely with Larnell.

"As to the engagement, though I sought your permission as Lizzie's father, the verbal contract was between the two of us. I would like to hear her wishes before I speak to it."

Lizzie took a deep breath and smiled tenderly as a single tear trickled down her cheek.

"I agreed to marry Bobby because I know him to be a man of honor, a man of courage, and a man who honors God and his convictions. I love him with all my heart—second only to God—and I believe he loves me the same way.

"He has done nothing to break our agreement, and he has done nothing to change my opinion. If anything, he has again demonstrated that all those things I believe about him are true. At this moment, I love him more than I ever have, and I see absolutely no reason for us to not become husband and wife.

"However, I am in full agreement that the engagement party should be canceled. Also, we need to cancel the wedding ceremony and reception here in Richmond. We will be married elsewhere, if Bobby will still have me. It will not be the social event of the summer. It will be a simple ceremony for us to express our vows before God. So Major Fearsithe, what do you think? Will you still marry me—even though I come from a complicated family?"

"I wouldn't marry anyone else!" I exclaimed. "And perhaps now we don't need to wait until June to get married!"

"Daddy, as to my assignment over Larnell's care, that is strictly up to the hospital administrators. However, I will be talking to them about resigning my commission from the Nursing Corps so I will be free to go where Bobby goes. So soon, the matter of my looking after Larnell will be a moot point.

"Allow me to add that I am proud of the way Bobby and Larnell have continued their friendship despite what they have faced in a world that hates a man simply because of the color of his skin. I pray that in our lifetime, the figurative and literal monuments to bigotry still prevalent across this land will be destroyed—and we become a world that is colorblind, just like these two men!"

≈

20

SATURDAY AFTERNOON, FEBRUARY 23 – SUNDAY, FEBRUARY 24, 1946

～

That afternoon, Larnell and I went looking for lodging. We discovered the Hotel Eggleston in the Jackson Ward area, which was also known as the "Harlem of the South." The hotel was one of only three available to colored people. Larnell found it suitable and reasonably priced. However, because of the segregation laws, I was not permitted to stay there.

I was still deciding whether to head back to Williamsport, so I found a room at the Hotel Richmond to stay in temporarily.

I returned the rental house keys to Arthur when I stopped by to see Lizzie that evening.

"How would you like to go see a movie tonight?" I asked her.

"With everything going on right now, you want to go see a movie?"

"I sure do," I replied. "I think it's just what we need. It will help us clear our heads for a couple of hours."

"What's showing?" Lizzie asked.

"The Bandit of Sherwood Forest with Cornel Wilde is showing at the Byrd Theater over on Cary Street," I told her. "It's about Robert of Nottingham, the son of Robin Hood, who comes to the aid of the beautiful Lady Catherine who is fleeing from the cruel regent."

"I don't know," Lizzie laughed, "it sounds too much like our story. You're Robert of Nottingham, I'm Lady Catherine, and my father is the cruel regent!"

"That's not true," I said, "your father isn't being cruel. He's just trying to protect his family and his business."

"But you wouldn't have done what he's doing," she countered.

"Maybe not," I agreed, "but I'm not in his shoes. And I've only lived in Richmond a few weeks. He's got a lot invested here. Besides, Larnell and I talked this afternoon. We really want to go into a business venture together —and there's no question that would be problematic here in Richmond.

"So, what do you say? Do you want to go to the movie?" I repeated.

"Are we sure the theater isn't owned by Senator Byrd?" Lizzie asked sarcastically.

"No, I already asked," I replied, smiling. "The theater was actually named in honor of his ancestor William Byrd II—a planter, lawyer, surveyor, and writer back when this country was still under British rule. But if you're going to avoid everything connected to the Byrd family, you'll probably have to move out of Virginia! So, what do you say—are we going to the movies?"

"Sure! Why not."

The Byrd turned out to be a humdinger. A Wurlitzer pipe organ rose from the orchestra pit to entertain the audience prior to the show. It was a swell setting with an eighteen-foot crystal chandelier, velvet drapes, and oil canvases hung throughout bearing images from Greek mythology.

However, I noticed it, too, seemed to be designed to segregate the races. I figured white people sat on the main floor and Negroes in the balcony. But when I realized there were no colored people in the theater, I asked about it. I was told they were not permitted in the Byrd—coloreds had their own separate theater in the city.

Yet another reminder of a harsh reality.

At least the movie took our minds off of our problems—for a couple hours anyway.

～

Although I wanted to attend church Sunday morning, I feared Lizzie's and my presence at First Baptist would merely stir up gossip. Lizzie's family did not plan to attend for the same reason. I regretted that because the Dodds had become more receptive to attending church since Lizzie's baptism.

Larnell and I had spotted Sixth Mount Zion Baptist Church while we were looking for a hotel Saturday and decided that was as good a place as any.

Since it was only a two-block walk for Larnell, we had planned to meet at the church at 1030 hours.

But when I arrived at the Dodd home to pick up Lizzie, she showed me a handwritten note delivered to their home earlier that morning:

> Dear Miss Elizabeth Dodd,
>
> God has not permitted me to have much peace since the events at your home Friday evening. I regret that you, your family, and those brave war heroes were subjected to that treatment. I am writing to ask if you would do me the kindness of conveying a message to Major Fearsithe and Captain Williams on my behalf.
>
> I doubt any of you plan to attend our worship service this morning, but I am personally inviting you and the two of them to please join us. I do not intend to single anyone out, but I would like them to hear the message that God has placed on my heart for this morning.
>
> I am quite aware this comes as more of a request than an invitation, but I pray you and they will do me the honor.
>
> Your servant,
> Pastor Theodore Adams

"Did you show this to your parents?" I asked.

"Yes, I did."

"Do they plan to attend?"

"They are still discussing it," Lizzie replied.

The two of us drove over to the Hotel Eggleston and caught Larnell just as he was coming out the door.

"I thought we were meeting at the church," he said looking perplexed. "Why the change of plans?"

"Because of this," I said as I handed him the note.

"What do you want to do?" I asked after he'd read it. "We can still head over to Sixth Mount Zion. After all, we're already here. But somehow I feel like we need to honor this pastor's request. I don't know what he has planned, but if the events of Friday night somehow shaped what he's going to preach today, then maybe we should hear it. But it's your call. Lizzie and I are going with you this morning—wherever you want to attend!"

"Do they even let colored people in the church?" Larnell asked.

"I honestly don't know," I responded. "But they plan to this morning. And we even received a handwritten request from the pastor. How often does that happen?"

Larnell nodded thoughtfully. "Then I guess we need to go and see what it's all about."

≈

To say we were the center of attention at church that morning was putting it mildly. Between our dress uniforms, our respective heights and military bearing, Larnell's facial injury, and his skin color, we were definitely hard to miss.

Some church members obviously knew what had happened Friday night, so before long the whispers started. A few braver folks walked up and welcomed us. We decided to sit in the back of the sanctuary so as not to call any more attention to ourselves.

As the choir led us in congregational singing, I realized Larnell had a beautiful baritone voice. I had never heard him sing before. Several folks glanced his way and nodded approvingly.

After a while, Pastor Adams took his place at the pulpit and said, "Please open your Bibles to Luke chapter ten, and let's read verses twenty-five through thirty-seven:

And behold, a certain lawyer stood up and tested Jesus, saying, "Teacher, what shall I do to inherit eternal life?"

Jesus said to him, "What is written in the law? What is your reading of it?"

So the lawyer answered and said, "'You shall love the Lord your God with all your heart, with all your soul, with all your strength, and with all your mind,' and 'your neighbor as yourself.'"

And Jesus said to him, "You have answered rightly; do this and you will live."

But the lawyer, wanting to justify himself, said to Jesus, "And who is my neighbor?"

Then Jesus answered and said: "A certain man went down from Jerusalem to Jericho, and fell among thieves, who stripped him of his clothing, wounded him, and departed, leaving him half dead. Now by chance a certain priest came down that road. And when he saw him, he passed by on the other side. Likewise a Levite, when he arrived at the place, came and looked, and passed by on the other side. But a certain Samaritan, as he journeyed, came where he was. And when he saw him, he had compassion. So he went to him and bandaged his wounds, pouring on oil and wine; and he set him on his own animal, brought him to an inn, and took care of him. On the next day, when he departed, he took out two denarii, gave them to the innkeeper, and said to him, 'Take care of him; and whatever more you spend, when I come again, I will repay you.' So which of these three do you think was neighbor to him who fell among the thieves?"

And the lawyer said, "He who showed mercy on him."

Then Jesus said to him, "Go and do likewise."[1]

"The lawyer in this passage was not coming to Jesus as a sincere seeker," the pastor told us. "He was an expert in the religious laws with an ulterior motive. The religious leaders had their own agenda, and it was built on their interpretation of the laws. The laws had become the means by which they were able to wield authority over the people. Jesus was a threat to that power, so they sent this lawyer to test Him, or perhaps even catch Him in a statement that would discredit Him.

"But Jesus took what the enemy intended for evil and turned it for good. A question intended to trip up Jesus was masterfully turned into one of the greatest lessons He would have us learn.

"Jesus never said the story of the Good Samaritan was a parable. It could well be the report of an actual occurrence that had happened to one or more of the people Jesus was addressing that day—perhaps the lawyer himself.

"In that day and time, great hostility existed between the Jews and the Samaritans, which dated back to when Israel split into two kingdoms. Prejudice had developed between the two peoples— very similar to the racial bigotry that exists today. The Jews felt they were superior to the Samaritans.

"A story that made the Jews look bad and the Samaritans look good would have angered many of the Jews. For Jesus to tell a story like this if it weren't true would have been risky. But let's not lose sight! Jesus knew everything about everyone. The same Jesus—who wrote in the dirt when religious leaders brought Him a woman caught in adultery—was able to use actual events in the lives of some of these men to teach a truth.

"Yes, quite possibly it was straight out of the life of this lawyer. Perhaps it is an experience straight out of some of our lives!

"The path between Jerusalem and Jericho was treacherous. It was a narrow, winding trail through some rocky and barren landscape. It had also become a 'high crime' area that neither the Roman soldiers nor the Jewish leaders cared enough about to police.

"A Jewish priest and a Jewish Levite were the first people to see the injured Jewish man lying along the roadside. The priest had been serving God at the temple all week, and he was anxious to get home. He had put in enough time ministering to others for one week.

"Also, perhaps he feared the robbers who had attacked this man were hiding in wait for the next person who stopped. He couldn't take that risk. Besides, the man was not a member of his synagogue. Why should he concern himself? So he went on his way.

"The Levite did exactly what the priest had done—nothing! It reminds us that such is the power of the bad example of a religious man.

"The fact that the 'hero' of this account was a Samaritan made the point even more poignant to the Jews. It was one thing if a Jew had stopped to help a Samaritan, but this was a Samaritan stopping to help a Jew … whom two other Jews had already passed by.

"The Samaritan showed love to someone who hated him. He risked his own life and spent his own money. He did not seek any credit or honor for his actions. Instead, he felt compassion and showed the wounded man mercy, expecting nothing in return.

"The lawyer wanted to have an intellectual discussion with Jesus about who was and was not his neighbor. But Jesus forced him to consider that the one in need was his neighbor regardless of who he was or where he was from.

"How easily do we allow who a man is or where he comes from prevent us from seeing him as our neighbor? Seeing him as our neighbor means getting involved personally, which requires us to get our hands dirty. We must allow ourselves to become inconvenienced. And there's a good possibility our efforts won't be appreciated by those who think or act like the priest and the Levite. The lawyer wanted to make the issue philosophical; Jesus made it practical!

"Ministering to the mistreated Jewish man cost the Samaritan two silver coins and some time, but not helping him cost the two Jewish religious leaders much more. They lost the opportunity to invest their God-given time and resources into a neighbor—one of God's creations. They also missed the opportunity to become better men and caring neighbors as they were created to be—and which they professed to be as followers of God.

"Surely, the most shameful thing of all was they chose to be a bad influence in a world that so desperately needed a good one. And I'm afraid too many others continue to do the same today.

"Jesus told us to love our neighbor as ourselves. Let's be sure we recognize who our neighbors are, and let's be sure we don't walk past them! Like Jesus said, 'Now go and do likewise!'"

Pastor Adams led us in a time of invitation as we sang "Have Thine Own Way, Lord." I'm not sure what kind of reaction he expected that morning— but the aisles didn't suddenly fill with people convicted by his sermon. In fact, no one walked forward to the altar. However, as people shuffled out of the sanctuary, I noticed several who appeared to be mulling over his message.

Racial discrimination had deep roots in many states, especially those in the South. It was unrealistic to think one sermon could make a dent—but it was a step in the right direction.

We waited in our pew until most everyone else had gone before we exited.

"Thank you, pastor, for inviting us to come," I said as Lizzie and I shook his hand at the door. "And thank you for your thoughtful words. Sometimes we just need to have our eyes opened to the injustice around us in order to make a change. And if enough of us make that belated discovery, someday real change for the better will occur."

"God bless you, pastor," Larnell said, "and keep preaching what God tells you to preach."

∾

---

[1] Luke 10:25-37 (NKJV)

21

MONDAY, FEBRUARY 25 – SATURDAY, MARCH 16, 1946

~

Over the next couple of days, the three of us decided we would all return to Williamsport. Lizzie submitted her resignation at the hospital effective Friday, March 15. She would look for a nursing position in Williamsport once we got settled.

She seemed to bear the disappointment with grace that she was no longer going to have the fairy tale princess wedding she had always envisioned. Her parents would not be hosting the social event that had been planned all her life. As a matter of fact, they would not be hosting any ceremonial event in Richmond.

Instead, we decided to be married in Pennsylvania, where my family and friends could attend. We discussed it by phone with my parents and they were thrilled to have the opportunity to help us plan the wedding. They had always regretted not having a daughter, but now they were going to have one—and all the joys that go with it.

We didn't see the need to prolong our engagement, so we began to discuss dates. Saturday, April 6, quickly, rose to the top of the list—after all, who wouldn't want to get married on 4-6-46? My parents agreed to contact Rev. Peterson to make sure he and Memorial Baptist Church were available.

Since there was no sense in my remaining in Richmond until mid-March, I set out for Williamsport on Wednesday morning, February 27. I would return to Richmond to collect Lizzie on March 15.

I hadn't realized how much I needed to see my parents until I pulled up to their house. After enjoying a delicious meal, we spent the rest of the night talking about what happened in Richmond. My mom and dad both struggled with what I had experienced. They couldn't understand how one race could treat another with such malice in this day and time. And they certainly didn't understand how bigotry could be allowed to control what people could and could not do.

"Don't people in Virginia understand that our founding fathers declared all men are created equal?" my father asked.

"Dad, the day I enlisted in the Army, I discovered few people function as if those words are true—regardless of where they were from. It may be more subtle here in the North than it is in places like Richmond, but deep down, it still exists. It controls all our lives to one degree or another.

"It dictates where we live, where we go to school, where we can work, and what we're allowed to do. It establishes our behaviors, our friendships, and even where we attend church. And the sad thing is, we've accepted it for so long that we've become accustomed to it.

"Like the preacher at First Baptist Church said this past Sunday: "How can we love one another like the Bible says if we refuse to talk to each other, care for each other, or acknowledge we are all the same in the eyes of our Creator?"

"I never thought of Williamsport as being racially divided, or myself as prejudiced, but you may be right, son," my dad replied. "There may be different degrees of prejudice, but at the end of the day, it's all wrong. How do we change it?"

"I know there are people trying, just like President Roosevelt did," I answered. "Larnell, Frank, Rob, and I were together in OCS because the president told the generals they had to try. It hasn't made much progress so far. But other people—both colored and white—are trying to make a difference.

"But lasting change must happen one person at a time until it results in an overwhelming wave that no one can stand against. And I've decided I want to be part of that wave."

"That makes sense, Bobby," Dad acknowledged, "and I'm proud of you. But that kind of change will take more than one lifetime. In the meantime, I don't understand how people like the Dodds would cave in to that way of thinking and not support their daughter and her fiancé."

"Because it is the ecosystem in which they live and operate," I replied. "And it has been the infrastructure for generations. It's how people live, work, and succeed. In many ways, it's how they breathe. Life exists and continues under these rules, and if you want to exist and continue, you follow them.

"I didn't realize until it was too late that I put Arthur Dodd in a position where he didn't have much choice. If he had reacted differently, it would have cost him everything he holds dear. From his perspective, the decisions he made were preferable to the havoc it would wreak if he didn't make them.

"Arthur and Myra are not bad people. They love their daughter, and I think they still love me. They want to see us succeed and be happy in our marriage. Privately, he has not retracted his blessing. They've already told us they plan to come here for our wedding. They just can't acknowledge our engagement publicly in Virginia society. They believe they must function within the rules set for them—and everyone else—by the powerbrokers who control them."

After my early morning run the next day, I stopped by to see Mr. Lundy.

"Bobby, I never expected to see you back here so soon," he remarked. "Are you here to visit your folks?"

"No, I'm actually moving back to town, and I wanted to see if you might have some work for me."

"I assume things didn't work out with that young woman you were going to marry?" he asked.

"Oh, no!" I exclaimed. "We're getting married April 6 right here in Williamsport. You'll be getting a wedding invitation. However, things didn't pan out in Richmond workwise. My future father-in-law and I realized we wouldn't be able to work together, so I resigned."

"Lizzie and I decided we're going to settle here—at least for now. I completely understand if you no longer have an opening in contractor sales. I just wanted to check first before I looked elsewhere. And I didn't want you to hear I was back in town and hadn't come by to see you."

"I'm glad you did, Bobby," he replied. "I'm sorry things didn't work out for you. But Richmond's loss is our gain. I still haven't found the right person for that position, so it's yours if you want it. I guess the Man upstairs was keeping it vacant for you! How soon can you start?"

"Is tomorrow too soon?"

"Not at all!" he replied. "I'll see you at 7 a.m."

Mom had confirmed that Rev. Peterson had April 6 open on his calendar, so I stopped by the church to see if there was anything else I needed to do.

"Welcome, Bobby," he said as I walked in. "Your mother tells me I will have the privilege of officiating the wedding for you and Elizabeth. She told me the date is April 6, but do you have a time?"

"Yes, we decided it would take place at noon, if that time works for you."

"That's perfect," he said. "Later in the afternoon or early evening tends to encroach on my Sunday sermon preparation time. I'll want to meet with you and Elizabeth for a couple of sessions before the wedding."

"Lizzie will be arriving in town on March 16," I answered, "so that should work just fine. We can schedule the dates after she gets here, if that's okay with you. One more thing, pastor. I'm new to all of this, so I don't know how it works, but I'm assuming we'll need the church organist."

"I will tell him to book it on his calendar, and you and Elizabeth can speak with him regarding specifics once she gets to Williamsport."

I thanked the pastor and set off for the Lycoming Hotel. My parents had suggested it as a possible location for the wedding luncheon following the ceremony. I was relieved that the hotel's Lucille Room was still available that afternoon and for a reasonable price. I put down a deposit and was pleased to report on my progress when I called Lizzie later that night. We both felt a peace about everything and knew God was ordering our steps.

I arrived at Lundy Lumber the next morning raring to go. As we discussed Mr. Lundy's vision for the new contractor sales division, he held up a hand to stop me.

"Bobby, if you're going to be one of my key executives, it's about time you started calling me Richard," he chuckled.

The next three weeks passed quickly as I settled into my new job. The demand for new homes in Williamsport, much like the rest of the country, was exploding. Residential construction had been depressed during the war due to shortages in materials and manpower; now there was pent-up demand. Add to that the returning GIs like me who were looking to get married, start a family, and make a home.

A number of new builders were starting up—and we were looking to take advantage of that demand and become their supplier of choice. As I looked over the company's book of business, I immediately noticed there were no Negro builders on the list.

"I never really thought about it," Richard replied when I asked him about it. We agreed to change that, and I told him I had just the man for the job.

Once again, God was going before us and making a way. A few days before I returned to Richmond, Larnell received word from his doctors that he was being released from their care on March 15—which meant he could travel to Williamsport with Lizzie and me! The fact his nurse was headed to the same city gave him added confidence.

I stopped by the Williams' home to make sure they had received Larnell's good news, and when Momma opened the door there was no doubt!

"I'm plannin' the biggest "welcome home" party there ever was," she excitedly announced. I promised her I would have him home by dinner time Saturday.

I made it to Richmond in time to pick up Lizzie at the hospital and give Larnell a ride to his hotel. It struck me that they were in two different places on the eve of our journey to Williamsport—one was headed home, and the other was leaving home. Though Lizzie was looking forward to our new adventure, I knew it was bittersweet. I tried to be sensitive to her feelings.

After we dropped off Larnell, we headed over to Lizzie's home. The Dodds had graciously invited me to spend the night. I was aware that in some circles that was even a risk for them. Cavendish met me at the door with a cheerful welcome. He seemed genuinely pleased to see me.

Arthur and Myra greeted me with a polite hug; Anne was much more demonstrative. Esther assured Lizzie and me that she had prepared some of our favorite dishes for the evening meal. My tastebuds were already salivating!

The evening was cordial. Myra asked about my parents; Arthur asked about my work. They both asked about the wedding plans and assured us they looked forward to being there. I once again extended my parents' invitation to host them in their home, but the Dodds declined saying they already had a reservation at the Lycoming Hotel.

"We will be arriving on the train Friday afternoon and departing on Sunday afternoon," Arthur said. "We can arrange our transportation to and from the train station, if necessary."

"Don't worry about that," Lizzie assured her parents. "One of us will be there to greet you at the train station."

Early the next morning, Lizzie and I picked up Larnell and set out for Williamsport. It had been over four years since Larnell left home to travel to Virginia for basic training—and much of that journey had been in the dark. He excitedly took in the sights as we passed by. He was particularly fascinated by the majestic height of the Washington Monument as it towered over the D.C. landscape.

"Bobby, did you know the monument was completed by the U.S. Army Corps of Engineers?" he asked. "They don't just build bridges and roads; they build structures that extend over 550 feet into the air. It gives me another reason to be proud that we were officers in the U. S. Army."

As we got closer to Pennsylvania, Larnell again wondered aloud about how his family was going to react to his physical appearance.

"Your momma is going to be so thrilled to see you that she won't even notice what you look like," I reassured him. "And the rest of them may notice momentarily, but their joy to have you back home will overshadow that in no time. Don't worry! Just give them time to adjust in their own way."

Larnell and I also discussed the new job opportunity that had developed at Lundy Lumber. I told him we'd be working together, and the job was his if he wanted it.

"But don't feel obligated," I cautioned. "If you want, you can come by the lumberyard early next week, and I can give you more details."

"That's probably best," Larnell agreed.

The sun was still shining when we arrived in Williamsport. As we pulled up in front of Larnell's home, the whole family streamed out the front door to greet him—led by his momma. Lizzie and I were touched as we watched the reunion unfold. It had been a long time coming—and I would dare say no one even noticed his disfigurement.

Momma came over and congratulated Lizzie on our engagement. She then insisted we join them for Larnell's celebration.

"I'm so sorry, we can't," I replied. "I promised my parents we'd spend the evening with them. We'll join you another time."

22

SUNDAY, MARCH 17 – SUNDAY MORNING, APRIL 7, 1946

≁

*W*e had barely exchanged pleasantries before my parents insisted Lizzie stay with them as their guest. We had planned for her to stay in a hotel; however, they would hear nothing of it. "No future daughter-in-law of ours is going to stay in a hotel!" That quickly settled the matter.

After my run the next morning, I was at the kitchen table enjoying a cup of coffee when Lizzie came downstairs and joined me. "What's on the schedule for today?" she asked.

"Well, first, Happy St. Patrick's Day to ya!" I greeted her in my best interpretation of an Irish brogue. "Since the holiday has fallen on Sunday this year, they held the parade yesterday. So you can cross that off your list, lassie!

"Otherwise, we'll go to worship this morning and come back home for Sunday dinner. Is there something you'd like to do after that?"

"How about you show me more of the city while we shop for an apartment to be our future home?" Lizzie replied.

While we were catching up with Rob Smith and his fiancée, Mary, after church, they mentioned an apartment they had seen but couldn't quite afford. "It's on Millionaires' Row!" Rob said.

"Well then, we certainly won't be able to afford it, either," Lizzie replied.

"Maybe you can afford this one," Rob continued. "Millionaires' Row is a stretch of Victorian mansions built by the lumber barons back in the 1800s. The owner of the company I work for owns a couple of the mansions and has turned each floor of them into individual apartments.

"The top floor features a one-bedroom apartment with the basics. They're not very big—so if you're looking to start a family really quick, it may not be for you—but they are plush. I can't afford it on a salesman's salary, but it might work for you.

"It's located at 967 West Fourth Street. Why don't you stop by and check it out? If you're interested, contact J.C. Winter at the Vallamont Planing Mill, down off West Third Street. Let him know I referred you!"

"We will do that, Rob," I said. "Thanks for the tip!"

The next day, Lizzie had no difficulty being hired as a nurse at the Williamsport Hospital. Her credentials from England and Richmond, combined with her many glowing letters of recommendation, more than spoke for her ability and character.

Meanwhile, Larnell paid me a visit at Lundy Lumber. Richard and I shared our vision for the business—including our intent to supply the Negro contracting community. We planned to provide quality lumber and building materials, delivered to the jobsite at reasonable prices, no matter the customer's race. I told Larnell he would be our first outside salesman, working for a base salary plus commission on sales.

"Larnell, a few weeks ago I told you we'd either set the building material business on fire in Pennsylvania or the steel business in Virginia," I said. "Today, we're taking that first step!"

And over the next two-and-a-half weeks, we began to do just that! However, on the afternoon of April 5, everything came to an abrupt halt … for Lizzie's and my wedding.

My mother and Lizzie had worked out almost all the details, with minimal help from the rest of us. They accomplished a wedding miracle in less than three weeks—including ordering a wedding gown, sending invitations, ordering flowers, selecting music, the cake, and the food.

Lizzie and I met Arthur, Myra, and Anne's train on Friday afternoon at the station. After stopping at the Lycoming Hotel for them to check in and freshen up, we all headed to the church for a brief rehearsal. Lizzie and I had chosen to have only two attendants—a maid of honor and a best man —so the logistics of the service were fairly simple.

Her father would walk her down the aisle and give her away. Anne, the maid of honor, would precede them. Pastor Peterson, my best man, and I would enter through a side door and wait for them at the front of the church. When Lizzie and I were planning our wedding, I realized the only person I wanted as my best man was Larnell, who had graciously accepted.

As I watched Arthur and Lizzie practice walking down the aisle, it dawned on me that Arthur and Larnell had not seen one another since that fateful birthday celebration six weeks earlier. Suddenly, the events of the past few weeks came rushing back to mind like the waters going over Niagara Falls.

I looked Arthur in the eye as he responded to Pastor Peterson's question: "Who gives this woman to be married to this man?"

"Her mother and I do," he answered.

At that moment, I was struck by the realization of how drastically our lives had been changed in a matter of forty-two days. No one outside our small wedding party could ever completely understand.

I was jolted back to the present as Lizzie turned to face me, placing both her hands in mine.

As soon as the rehearsal concluded, my parents hosted a dinner in their home for the wedding party, including Pastor Peterson and his wife, and the organist Olaf Seybert and his wife. I was pleased to see how well everyone seemed to enjoy one another's company, including—to my surprise—Arthur and Larnell.

Lizzie joined her parents and sister at the hotel that night, so they could enjoy some family time together, and in order to ensure that she and I did not see one another on our wedding day before she walked down the aisle. Given all that had transpired in the past several weeks, I was glad they could have that time together.

I spent the evening with my parents as they reminisced about their engagement and wedding ceremony. I never tired of hearing my father tell the story of how God had used a young woman in Portland to bring him to his senses about returning to Williamsport and marrying my mother. It reminded me of how God seizes our attention to transform our pursuits into His intended discoveries—and each of those discoveries is for our good, the good of those around us, and His glory!

The sky was clear, and the temperature was crisp when I got up for my early morning run. I was even earlier than usual—probably due to the butterflies in my stomach! I was preparing to marry the woman I knew God had created just for me. I couldn't wait for us to begin our lives together as husband and wife.

Larnell arrived to drive me to the church about an hour before the wedding. He and I had become brothers. We knew we would always have each other's back. And I was grateful he was walking with me each and every step this day.

Once we arrived at the church, I spent the next half hour wearing a hole in the carpet as I paced back and forth. Pastor Peterson came in the room and tried to lighten the mood. When I heard Olaf begin playing the prelude music, the pastor and Larnell both prayed over me.

Soon the moment arrived. I followed the pastor into the sanctuary with Larnell at my six, both of us wearing our dress uniforms. Though I did not have a sense of foreboding, once again my nerves were as much engaged as the day I was about to land on the French African shore. Fortunately, however, the expressions on the faces of the people sitting in the pews in front of me were much more encouraging.

The church was decorated with an array of Easter lilies, white flowers, and green palms. White cathedral tapers cast a soft glow despite the sun radiating through the stained-glass windows.

I glanced around the room at all those who had come to celebrate this day with Lizzie and me. I noticed a small tear making its way down my mother's cheek as she smiled at me from the front row. Myra was across the aisle from my parents looking off into the distance. I wondered if she were picturing this day as it might have been.

Behind my parents sat Momma, Clovis, and Rebecca. In the past few months, they too had become my family, and I am certain they would say I had become their second son. Behind them sat friends from school, work, and church. Their bright smiles let me know they had been cheering me on long before I realized it.

I don't believe I had ever truly realized how lovely Anne was until she started down the aisle. I was amazed at how much she and Lizzie looked alike. My new sister-in-law had never wavered in her support of Lizzie and me throughout the recent ordeal. Her fierce loyalty and strength of character had been a source of encouragement to us both.

Suddenly, Olaf started playing the "Wedding March."[1] I strained to catch my first glimpse of my bride as she and her father stepped into view. As they slowly made their way down the aisle, I admired the beautiful white gown Lizzie had chosen, together with the fingertip veil that was covering her face.

I momentarily turned my attention to Arthur and saw the look of love and pride he exuded for his eldest daughter. Though I may always question the decision he made that weekend in February, I would never doubt his love for his daughter.

As they stood next to me, I was finally able to look into Lizzie's eyes. I remembered the day I first looked into them as I chided her from my hospital bed—and the way she had disarmed me every day since then with her gaze. I think I may have fallen in love with her that very first day.

Pastor Peterson began the ceremony, but I couldn't tell you much of what he said. However, I do recall the following:

"Robert and Elizabeth, marriage is more than an institution. As followers of Christ, we hold to the belief that God views marriage as a sacred covenant between the two of you before Him. As such, it is not to be entered into lightly. It is an exclusive, lifelong relationship—freely chosen —and inseparably forged.

"It is built on trust and selflessness. It is based on unlimited responsibility—not on limited liability. It is a commitment that cannot be broken if new circumstances occur, or even by mutual consent. It is a commitment that is bound in complete faithfulness and uncompromised permanence.

"The famous playwright Thornton Wilder recently wrote a play titled, The Skin of Our Teeth. In the second act, Mrs. Maggie Antrobus says to her husband, Mr. George Antrobus:

'I didn't marry you because you were perfect. I didn't even marry you because I loved you. I married you because you gave me a promise. That promise made up for your faults. And the promise I gave you made up for mine. Two imperfect people got married and it was the promise that made the marriage. And when our children were growing up, it wasn't a house that protected them; and it wasn't our love that protected them—it was that promise.'" [2]

That promise was memorialized through the solemn vows and rings we exchanged that day. But when the pastor instructed us to seal our promise with a kiss, I must confess I had never before thought of a kiss as a seal. It became one for us that day, and each kiss ever since has been a renewal of that seal—and a reminder of that promise.

The wedding luncheon that followed at the Lycoming Hotel was something of a blur. I know pictures were taken, hugs were given, food was eaten, and cake was cut. I also remember, despite the photographer's prodding, that Lizzie and I resisted jamming cake into each other's mouth. I walked away thinking we had both passed that first test!

Once the cake had been served, the toasts had been delivered, and the bouquet and garter had been caught by the hopeful future bride and groom to be, Lizzie and I dashed through the hotel's front doors amidst a shower of rice. Larnell drove us away in my Buick as my new wife and I waved at the well-wishers from the rear seat.

We had decided to postpone our honeymoon trip to New York City until the fall. Lizzie had just recently begun her job at the hospital, and I was still early in my new venture at Lundy. So, I had arranged for us to stay in the honeymoon suite at the Lycoming.

Larnell ceremoniously drove us around the block, then we reentered the hotel through the secondary entrance on William Street. The hotel staff helped us sneak to our suite out of the view of our unsuspecting guests.

After a memorable night, we met Arthur, Myra, and Anne for a quiet morning breakfast. They had agreed to attend worship with us that morning, and we didn't want to miss that opportunity. The Memorial Baptist Church congregation was somewhat perplexed to see Lizzie and me show up the day after our wedding!

Since it was two weeks until Easter, Pastor Peterson was preaching through a series of messages in the Gospel of Mark. That Sunday morning, he read from the tenth chapter:

> As Jesus was starting out on His way to Jerusalem, a man came running up to Him, knelt down, and asked, "Good Teacher, what must I do to inherit eternal life?" Jesus answered, "You know the commandments: 'You must not murder. You must not commit adultery. You must not steal. You must not testify falsely. You must not cheat anyone. Honor your father and mother.'"

> "Teacher," the man replied, "I've obeyed all these commandments since I was young."
> Looking at the man, Jesus felt genuine love for him. "There is still one thing you haven't done," He told him. "Go and sell all your possessions and give the money to the poor, and you will have treasure in heaven. Then come, follow Me."

At this the man's face fell, and he went away sad, for he had many possessions.[3]

The pastor continued, "Throughout this series of messages, we have seen many people following Jesus. Most followed Him from a distance seeking what was in it for them—a miracle, a meal, even money and prestige. A smaller number followed Him closely and intimately because they believed and surrendered their lives to Him.

"Many who followed from a distance turned away—rejecting His statements that He came from heaven and rejecting that He is the Son of God. Some rebuffed Jesus because He threatened their power and position.

"But some actually came to the feet of Jesus. And in each of those instances, their lives were forever changed. They were healed. Their sins were forgiven. They experienced the love and the touch of the Master. Only one ever knelt at His feet and walked away feeling worse than when he had come. That man's encounter, which we read about today, is not only recorded by Mark, but also by Matthew and Luke.

"Matthew tells us he was a young man. Luke tells us he was a religious leader, in a position of authority. All three writers tell us he was very wealthy with many possessions. From all outward appearances, he had everything going for him.

"Unlike most religious leaders who questioned Jesus, this young man did not demonstrate a deceptive motive. He showed no sign of trying to entrap Jesus in another pharisaical plot. Rather, he came seeking Jesus with an attitude similar to Nicodemus's.

"He was a student of the Law—quite possibly a teacher himself. Along the way, through what he heard or witnessed firsthand, he came to respect Jesus as a Teacher—one who teaches with authority. So he came to Jesus with a sincere question: 'What must I do (or what good deed must I do) to inherit eternal life?'

"When Jesus specifically listed several commandments, the young man replied that he had obeyed them all since his youth. He had the view—like so many today—that he could do something to merit eternal life. But if we compare this list to the complete list of the ten commandments found in the twentieth chapter of Exodus, we notice that these are only the fifth through tenth commandments. This grouping speaks to how we relate to others around us.

"But the first four commandments address how we relate to God. Jesus was about to reveal to the young man that eternal life is the result of our relationship with God and not what we have done (or not done) for others. The true test was how he responded to Jesus's final statement: 'Go and sell all your possessions and give the money to the poor, and you will have treasure in heaven. Then come, follow Me.'

"The issue was not the young man's riches; the issue was that he valued his riches over a relationship with God. And he did not see himself as a condemned sinner before a holy God. He thought his superficial good works would merit favor with God.

"That is where many of us stumble. We value riches, or possessions, or position, or other relationships over a relationship with God. John, in his Gospel, writes that 'God so loved the world....'(4) Mark tells us here that Jesus felt genuine love for this young man. The Father and the Son have first loved us. As John writes, 'We love Him, because He first loved us.'(5)

"But when we refuse to love Him with our whole heart, soul, and mind—when we refuse to surrender everything else in our lives to Him—we walk away sad, we walk away empty, we walk away incomplete, and we walk away unfulfilled, just like this rich young ruler.

"No matter what else he possessed, there was a void in his life that would never be filled apart from one thing—a loving relationship with his heavenly Father. Jesus didn't plead with him. He spoke the truth to him in love. Then it was up to the young man to decide.

"And that is true for each one of us today. No matter what else we possess, there is a void in our lives that will never be filled apart from one thing—a loving relationship with our Lord.

"Jesus won't plead with us either. He has spoken His truth to us in love. And it is up to each of us to decide."

---

[1] Wedding March by Mendelssohn

[2] Excerpt from THE SKIN OF OUR TEETH by Thornton Wilder. Copyright © 1942 by The Wilder Family LLC. Reprinted by arrangement with The Wilder Family LLC and The Barbara Hogenson Agency, Inc. All rights reserved. To learn more about Thornton Wilder, see www.Thornton-Wilder.com

[3] Mark 10:17, 19-22 (ESV)

[4] John 3:16 (NLT)

[5] 1 John 4:19 (NLT)

23

SUNDAY AFTERNOON, APRIL 7, -- SUNDAY, APRIL 21, 1946

~

*A*fter church, Lizzie and I took her family out for dinner at the Old Corner Hotel. William Hopler, a friend of mine from high school, was the owner. It was a quiet place where I knew we wouldn't be disturbed.

I ordered for everyone—chicken and waffles, one of my favorites— prepared the Pennsylvania Dutch way instead of Southern style. I wanted my in-laws to experience a new cuisine. As we waited for our food, I asked Arthur what he thought about the pastor's message.

"It was quite interesting," he replied. "I've never given it much thought, but my views probably align with the rich, young man—as long as I live by the rules, God will let me into heaven when I die. The preacher, however, seems to think that's not enough. What do you think?"

"I believe there is only one Man qualified to provide us with an irrefutable answer to that question—Jesus. Only the Son of God could tell us decisively how to have a relationship with God the Father. Jesus repeatedly gave the same answer to everyone who asked: '*I am the Way, the Truth, and the Life. No one can come to the Father except through Me.*'[1]

"He also tells us He came that we might have abundant life, fulfilling life, as well as eternal life. And it doesn't start when we die; we can have that life here and now. It doesn't depend on our wealth, our achievements, or our success. It depends on our faith in Jesus."

"You obviously agree with what the pastor was saying," Arthur responded.

"So do I, Daddy," Lizzie chimed in. "That's why I was baptized that day at First Baptist Church. I was publicly declaring my belief in Jesus and that He is the only way to heaven. Only through Him can we be forgiven for everything wrong we have ever done."

"Elizabeth, what did you do when you made that decision?" Anne asked. "I didn't see you selling your possessions like Jesus told the man in the story to do."

"No, I didn't sell all my possessions, Anne," Lizzie replied. "I did the greater thing that Jesus was talking about. You see, we can sell all our possessions thinking that will make us good enough. But if we continue to believe our good deeds and the selflessness we think we are demonstrating are the answer, then we're still not trusting in Jesus. We have to trust Him—and Him alone. He'll tell us if we need to give everything away, or something away, or nothing away. The question is, are we allowing Him to lead our lives?

"Bobby and I have come to the place that we trust in Jesus alone. It doesn't really matter where we live, how big our house is, or what we're doing—as long as we obey what He tells us to do."

"Does God talk to you then?" Anne asked with a skeptical look.

"In a way, yes," Lizzie answered. "Not like you and I are sitting here talking; but rather, through His Word in the Bible, through the counsel of other Christians, or through the prompting of the Holy Spirit. You've heard that still, small voice in your heart, Anne. I know you have, because you've told me. You knew when you were supposed to do something, because it was the right thing to do. Likewise, you knew when you shouldn't do something, because God's Spirit convicted you it was wrong."

"I think we've all heard that voice," Myra interjected. "And I know I've felt pretty lousy when I didn't obey. Like the way I felt when we abandoned our own daughter and future son-in-law because of whom they had chosen to be their friend. I regret that we listened to what everyone around us was telling us to do—instead of doing what was right. Only that still small voice speaks the real truth."

We paused our conversation while the waiter served our meal.

"Arthur, do you mind if I say the blessing before we eat?" I asked.

"No, not at all," he replied.

"Thank You, God, for this food and the nourishment You provide through it. And thank You for Your Word and the Truth and Light You give us through it. Help us to allow that Truth and Light to guide us, just like we allow the food to nourish us. In Jesus's name, Amen!"

As we began to eat our meal, the conversation changed.

"This is different from any chicken and waffles I've ever had," Anne commented after her first mouthful. "This is like chicken and dumplings, only the waffles are the dumplings."

"That's a great way to explain it, Anne," I agreed. "It's kind of like explaining the Gospel to someone who doesn't believe. It helps when you explain it in a way that others understand."

"Yes, I agree," Myra commented. "For example, Elizabeth, what you and Bobby have been telling us, combined with what the preacher said this morning, makes more sense than anything I've ever been told about Jesus. I believe I now understand what it means to believe in and follow Him."

"Then the next question is, what are you going to do about it, Mother?" Lizzie asked. "Are you going to make that decision and follow Him—or are you going to do what the rich man did and walk away?"

Everyone at the table got quiet as we waited for Myra's response.

"I'm going to follow Jesus!" she said, smiling through tears of joy.

"So am I!" Anne exclaimed. "What do I have to do?"

No one looked at Arthur for fear he would feel pressured to respond as well.

"Well, ladies, the Bible says we must confess our sins, repent, and ask God for forgiveness. We are able to do that because Jesus died for our sins on the cross. We must follow Him—not only in word, but, more importantly, in deed. It's not a matter of repeating some words and praying a simple prayer; you have to mean it with your whole heart. It's like the pledge Elizabeth and I made to each other yesterday; it's a lifetime commitment.

"And you can accept Jesus anywhere: in this restaurant, in your hotel room, at home, or standing in the middle of the street! It doesn't matter. The only thing God requires is that you tell others about His Son.

"When you return home, you need to tell Pastor Adams about your decision and ask him to baptize you. It tells us in the Bible that's the first thing we need to do. Being lowered into the water symbolizes His death on the cross and burial in the tomb. Being raised out of the water symbolizes joining Him in His resurrection and following Him."

Anne decided to pray right there in the middle of the restaurant; so did Myra. Arthur eventually spoke up and told us he wanted to think about it a little more. I told him if he had any questions, he could reach out to me and Elizabeth, Pastor Adams, or another Christian he felt comfortable with —any of us would be happy to help him find the answers.

We continued talking and laughing until the middle of the afternoon when it was time to take them to the train station. Our farewell that afternoon was with mixed emotions. We were sad to say goodbye, but we had many fond memories of our weekend together. Best of all, Lizzie and I were overjoyed about the decisions Myra and Anne had made.

As my new bride and I drove home, I reflected on how much things had shifted over the past couple of months. The cloud covering my memories since my birthday party was now replaced by exhilaration over Anne and Myra's newfound faith. And though the consequences of that night remained, changed hearts were a step in the right direction. And who knows what will happen down the road when we follow Jesus!

One week later, Anne called to tell us she and her mother were being baptized Easter morning. Our hearts leaped when she asked if we would come to Richmond to share in that special moment. We were still getting settled in our new apartment, and our jobs didn't allow us much time off —but there was no doubt we were going.

"Of course, we will be there!" we replied. "We'll see you Saturday afternoon."

Anne then presented one other request. I told her I didn't know if it was possible, but I would do my best to make it happen.

We boarded the train bright and early Saturday morning, April 20, and pulled into the Richmond station at 4:20 p.m. Cavendish greeted us at the station and chauffeured us to the Dodd residence. He assured us that evening's meal was for family only, so we looked forward to our time together.

He also shared that Mr. Dodd had given him specific instructions not to make any interim stops, but to bring us directly to Monument Avenue. Cavendish delivered us to the house in record time.

He then instructed us to enter the house through the front door instead of the family entry. That seemed a little odd, but I was even more puzzled when Arthur was the one who greeted us. That was unusual, even for family arrivals. However, Lizzie didn't give it a second thought. She immediately embraced her father, followed by hugs for Myra and Anne.

I followed suit by giving each of them a hug which they affectionately returned.

But my biggest surprise came when our fellow traveler, Larnell, went to shake Arthur's hand. Arthur ignored the extended hand and welcomed him with a warm embrace.

"Welcome to our home," Arthur told him. "Thank you for accepting our invitation; I would have understood if you hadn't. And please forgive me for the lack of hospitality and respect I showed you on your last visit."

"I know you were under a great deal of pressure then, Mr. Dodd," Larnell replied. "I should have been more understanding of the difficult situation in which we placed you and bowed out graciously that night."

"You are most kind, Larnell," Arthur responded, "and please call me Arthur. I have come to realize we are family, and family does not stand on ceremony. Please come in."

We enjoyed a delightful meal prepared by Esther, though I was careful not to offer too much praise. I didn't want to offend my new wife and her recent cooking attempts.

"Bobby, I hope you didn't have high expectations regarding Elizabeth's culinary skills when you proposed marriage," Arthur said with a chuckle. "There was a reason we only permitted Esther to prepare your meals when you stayed with us," he added to everyone's amusement.

"Lizzie is making great strides," I replied, coming to her defense. "We are now enjoying a wide variety of soups prepared from a can, and hopefully soon, we will be able to dine on boiled eggs." This last remark caused the entire room to dissolve into laughter, including Lizzie.

After dinner, Myra and Anne told us about their discussions with Pastor Adams as well as his recommendations regarding their continued discipleship. They seemed excited about their journey of faith, and we were pleased for them. Arthur, however, remained silent throughout that conversation.

At the end of the evening, Larnell asked if Cavendish could drive him to the hotel, or if he should arrange for a taxi.

"You won't be needing a hotel this evening," Arthur replied, "since you will be staying here as our guest. Cavendish will show you to your room."

I was amazed at the transformation I witnessed in the Dodd home that evening. But, then again, There was no denying the evening had been filled with surprises, but I had come to expect them every time I visited the Dodd's! I was learning that visiting as family would not prove to be an exception.

It was a gorgeous Easter morning as I ran along Monument Avenue. The spring flowers were vibrant, and the coating of pollen on parked cars was evidence that everything was in full bloom.

After a light breakfast, we all headed to the church, including Arthur. However, when Larnell, Lizzie, and I entered the sanctuary, Lizzie's dad was nowhere to be found. It crossed my mind that maybe he still didn't want to be seen in church sitting with a colored man. I sighed, wondering if we'd ever get past such nonsense.

Just as they'd done previously, some members of the congregation warmly greeted Larnell and me, while others scowled at us from a distance. Pastor Adams, dressed in a white gown, announced from the baptistry that five were being baptized this morning.

The first to join the pastor was Anne, wearing a similar white robe.

"Anne, have you repented of your sins and placed your faith in Jesus Christ, and Him alone, for your salvation?" Pastor Adams asked.

"I have."

"Then, upon your profession of faith," he said, as he lowered her under the water then raised her back up, "I baptize you now, my sister, in the name of the Father, the Son, and the Holy Spirit. You are buried with Christ in baptism, and raised to walk in new life with Him."

A chorus of amens resounded throughout the congregation.

As Anne exited the baptistery, Myra entered. The pastor asked her the same question, then baptized her. Amens again echoed through the room.

Nothing could have prepared me for the next person to be baptized. It was Arthur! Swallowing a lump in my throat, I peeked over at Lizzie to see tears streaming down her face. Arthur professed his faith and was baptized. And this time the amens were even louder. It began to dawn on people they had just witnessed the Dodd family—one of the most prominent families in Richmond—publicly profess their faith in Jesus.

The surprises did not stop there. The next person to enter the baptismal waters was Esther, followed by Cavendish.

"On several occasions in the book of Acts we read where entire households come to faith in Jesus at the same time," Pastor Adams remarked. "Today you have borne witness to another example of that. Arthur and Myra Dodd, their daughter Anne, and their household staff, Esther and Cavendish, were all baptized today. And the Dodds' eldest daughter, Elizabeth, was baptized three months ago in these same waters. Praise God He is still bringing households to salvation in Him!"

We had much to celebrate at dinner that Easter Sunday. We expressed gratitude for our Lord's resurrection following His death on the cross. And we praised Him for answering prayers for this family's salvation. Esther and Cavendish joined us at the table for the meal. For the first time, those seated around that table were brothers and sisters in Christ.

Though we didn't want this joyful time to end, Larnell, Lizzie, and I had to depart that afternoon for Williamsport. But not before we realized that each one of us had experienced a belated discovery during recent months.

For most of us, it had been the discovery and acceptance of our salvation through Jesus Christ. For all of us, it was a recognition that regardless of our skin color, we are all created equal—in God's image.

The world is full of people who have yet to make those discoveries. Most of the time, it occurs one life at a time. But sometimes, the Spirit of God moves in such a way that it happens to an entire household—just like we had witnessed with the Dodd family.

---

[1] John 14:6 (NLT)

EPILOGUE

~

$\mathcal{T}$wo and a half weeks later, on Wednesday, May 8, 1946, the countries making up the Allied forces celebrated Victory in Europe (VE) Day. Cities across the U.S. came to a standstill as parades filled the streets, politicians gave speeches, soldiers shared stories, and those still grieving remembered their deceased loved ones. Though the reminders of war were fresh in our hearts and minds, I don't think time could ever truly diminish the memories of those who served.

Arthur approached me the following summer about coming back to work for him. He assured me we could still reach the goal we had shared. But I realized Richmond was not yet ready for the changes needed to achieve our vision. I was confident it would one day, but not this day.

Besides, God was blessing my partnership with Larnell; our business was steadily growing. So were our families! Lizzie and I were parents of a baby boy, Robert Eugene Fearsithe III, whom we nicknamed Rob; and Larnell and his wife are expecting a little one due in six months. And our circle continued to grow, as God introduced us to "neighbors" we had never met

—near and far, light and dark, young and old. He was teaching us to love each one.

Larnell and I often talk about how the pride and relief we all felt after the war will one day be forgotten. A new generation will soon come along with memories of their own wars, pushing older conflicts to the side. The household names of one era will eventually be replaced by those of another. The Greatest Generation (born 1901-1924), like me, and the Silent Generation (born 1925-1945) will be pushed out of the way by our children, the Baby Boomers (born 1946-1964).

Each generation will have its own heroes, music, clothing styles, and their own perspectives on what is important, what should be preserved, and what needs to be honored.

As I look back over my life, I have memories that I will never forget: the day I met Lizzie, our wedding day, the birth of my son. But there are others I wish I could forget: the images of wartime's barbarity, the sadistic atrocities of concentration and prison camps, the acts of wickedness perpetrated by one race of people on another. I wish racism had never been seen as normal, practiced as acceptable, or fostered as admissible.

I'd like to turn back the clock and undo all the pain, inhumanity, and suffering that Satan has used to manipulate and lie to mankind. And I wish the hatred that causes daily death and destruction would once and for all be eradicated.

Sometimes, I even wish I could go back to the very beginning and stop Eve from taking that first bite of the forbidden fruit. I'd like to think she would have chosen differently if she'd known what her disobedience would set in motion. But, would she? That's the mystery of belated discoveries. Would they have caused us to act or think differently if we'd discovered them in time? Would that have changed the course? Would it change the outcome?

In my pursuit to discover, I know three things to be fact:

- I am not the Creator and have no power to wish anything away.

- Our Creator has the power to change. He sent His Son to suffer so He might have the power to save. He promised to make all things new and has everything in place to accomplish that. Though there will still be eternal changes once He returns, there are immediate changes we can experience in our lives in the here and now.

- Our Savior sent His Spirit to accomplish the work through us that He intends to be completed before His return. In order to carry that out, He has placed within us the fruit of His Spirit: love, joy, peace, patience, kindness, goodness, faithfulness, gentleness, and self-control. He did not dwell within us at our physical birth, but rather when we were born again. In that respect, His presence is a belated discovery given at salvation to accomplish God's purpose in His timing for His glory.

One day there will be no war. One day there will be no bigotry and hatred. Until then, be on the lookout for the next discovery He has for you—belated or not!

⌒

PLEASE HELP ME BY LEAVING A REVIEW!

i would be very grateful if you would leave a review of this book. Your feedback will be helpful to me in my future writing endeavors and will also assist others as they consider picking up a copy of the book.

To leave a review:

Go to: amazon.com/dp/1956866345

Or scan this QR code using your camera on your smartphone:

Thanks for your help!

∾

"THE PARABLES" SERIES

An Elusive Pursuit (Book 1)

Twenty-three year old Eugene Fearsithe boarded a train on the first day of April 1912 in pursuit of his elusive dream. Little did he know where the journey would take him, or what . . . and who . . . he would discover along the way.

Available on Amazon

~

A Belated Discovery (Book 2)

Nineteen year old Bobby Fearsithe enlisted in the army on the fifteenth day of December 1941 to fight for his family, his friends, and his neighbors. Along the way, he discovered just who his neighbor truly was.

Available on Amazon

~

AVAILABLE IN HARDCOVER, PAPERBACK, LARGE PRINT, AUDIO, AND FOR KINDLE ON AMAZON.

Scan this QR code using your camera on your smartphone to see the entire series.

For more information, go to *kenwinter.org* or *wildernesslessons.com*

"THE CALLED" SERIES

Stories of these ordinary men and women called by God to be used in extraordinary ways.

A Carpenter Called Joseph (Book 1)

A Prophet Called Isaiah (Book 2)

A Teacher Called Nicodemus (Book 3)

A Judge Called Deborah (Book 4)

A Merchant Called Lydia (Book 5)

A Friend Called Enoch (Book 6)

A Fisherman Called Simon (Book 7)

A Heroine Called Rahab (Book 8)

A Witness Called Mary (Book 9)

A Cupbearer Called Nehemiah (Book 10)

A Follower Called Mark (Book 11)

A Psalmist Called Asaph (Book 12) - Coming soon

AVAILABLE IN PAPERBACK, LARGE PRINT, AND FOR KINDLE ON AMAZON.

ALSO, A **DISCUSSION GUIDE** IS AVAILABLE AS A RESOURCE **FOR YOUR SMALL GROUP OR BOOK CLUB** AS YOU DISCUSS EACH OF THE BOOKS. AVAILABLE ON AMAZON IN PRINT OR FOR YOUR KINDLE.

Scan this QR code using your camera on your smartphone to see the entire series.

ALSO BY KENNETH A. WINTER

THROUGH THE EYES

(a series of biblical fiction novels)

Through the Eyes of a Shepherd (Shimon, a Bethlehem shepherd)

Through the Eyes of a Spy (Caleb, the Israelite spy)

Through the Eyes of a Prisoner (Paul, the apostle)

THE EYEWITNESSES

(a series of biblical fiction short story collections)

For Christmas/Advent

Little Did We Know – the advent of Jesus — for adults

Not Too Little To Know – the advent – ages 8 thru adult

For Easter/Lent

The One Who Stood Before Us – the ministry and passion of Jesus — for adults

The Little Ones Who Came – the ministry and passion – ages 8 thru adult

LESSONS LEARNED IN THE WILDERNESS SERIES

(a non-fiction series of biblical devotional studies)

The Journey Begins (Exodus) – Book 1

The Wandering Years (Numbers and Deuteronomy) – Book 2

Possessing The Promise (Joshua and Judges) – Book 3

Walking With The Master (The Gospels leading up to Palm Sunday) – Book 4

Taking Up The Cross (The Gospels – the passion through ascension) – Book 5

Until He Returns (The Book of Acts) – Book 6

ALSO AVAILABLE AS AUDIOBOOKS

THE CALLED series

A Carpenter Called Joseph

A Prophet Called Isaiah

A Teacher Called Nicodemus

A Judge Called Deborah

A Merchant Called Lydia

A Friend Called Enoch

A Fisherman Called Simon

A Heroine Called Rahab

A Witness Called Mary

A Cupbearer Called Nehemiah

A Follower Called Mark

∾

THROUGH THE EYES series

Through the Eyes of a Shepherd

Through the Eyes of a Spy

Through the Eyes of a Prisoner

∾

Little Did We Know

Not Too Little to Know

∾

THE PARABLES series

An Elusive Pursuit

A Belated Discovery

∾

ACKNOWLEDGMENTS

I do not cease to give thanks for you ....
Ephesians 1:16 (ESV)

… my partner and best friend, LaVonne,
for choosing to trust God as we walk together with Him in this faith
adventure;

… my family,
for your continuing love, support and encouragement;

… Sheryl,
for your partnership in the work;

… Scott,
for using the gifts God has given you;

… a precious group of advance readers,
who encourage and challenge me in the journey;

… and most importantly,
the One who goes before me in all things
– my Lord and Savior Jesus Christ!

∼

ABOUT THE AUTHOR

Ken Winter is a follower of Jesus, an extremely blessed husband, and a proud father and grandfather – all by the grace of God. His journey with Jesus has led him to serve on the pastoral staffs of two local churches – one in West Palm Beach, Florida and the other in Richmond, Virginia – and as the vice president of mobilization of an international missions organization.

Today, Ken continues in that journey as a full-time author, teacher and speaker. You can read his weekly blog posts at kenwinter.blog and listen to his weekly podcast at kenwinter.org/podcast.

And we proclaim Him, admonishing every man and teaching every man with all wisdom, that we may present every man complete in Christ. And for this purpose also I labor, striving according to His power, which mightily works within me.
(Colossians 1:28-29 NASB)

PLEASE JOIN MY READERS' GROUP

Please join my Readers' Group in order to receive updates and information about future releases, etc.

Also, i will send you a free copy of *The Journey Begins* e-book — the first book in the *Lessons Learned In The Wilderness* series. It is yours to keep or share with a friend or family member that you think might benefit from it.

It's completely free to sign up. i value your privacy and will not spam you. Also, you can unsubscribe at any time.

Go to kenwinter.org to subscribe.

Or scan this QR code using your camera on your smartphone:

～